'You've bought a bank?' she repeated in disbelief.

'Yes, Alice. I own it. You want to know why I didn't tell you that either? Habit, I guess—it's become second nature to me to play down my wealth. It tends to attract the wrong kind of women.'

Didn't he realise that she'd loved him when he'd had nothing—did that *count* for nothing?

'You didn't trust me enough to tell me something like that?' she questioned slowly. 'Like I really would have cared about your money?'

'It was a misjudgement,' he said heavily.

'Too right it was, Kyros. One misjudgement too many.'

'But now that this is all out in the open,' he said slowly, 'surely you can see the benefits of our marriage?'

'You mean our bizarre mockery of a marriage?'

He shook his dark head impatiently. 'Think about it, Alice. I need a woman in my life,' he said deliberately. 'And you fulfil my needs more than anyone else.' His voice softened. 'You always did. You get to enjoy all the things that my wealth can provide for you,' he said. 'Every day can be like it was yesterday. I have a boat we can sail—a plane we can fly. We can island-hop on one of my helicopters.' His lips curved into a smile. 'There will be no more scrimping and saving and making do—you shall have whatever you want, Alice.'

Except the thing which most eluded her—his love.

Modern™ Romance

presents a brand-new duet by star author

SHARON KENDRICK

The Greek Billionaires' Brides

*possessed by two Greek billionaire brothers—
as mistresses, as wives…*

Power, pride and passion—
divided by bitter rivalry, discover how
only the love and passion of two women can
reunite these wealthy, successful brothers.

Book 1:
THE GREEK TYCOON'S BABY BARGAIN
on sale May 2008

Book 2:
THE GREEK TYCOON'S CONVENIENT WIFE
on sale July 2008

THE GREEK TYCOON'S CONVENIENT WIFE

BY
SHARON KENDRICK

MILLS & BOON
Pure reading pleasure

First published in Great Britain 2008
Harlequin Mills & Boon Limited,
Eton House, 18-24 Paradise Road, Richmond, Surrey TW9 1SR

© Sharon Kendrick 2008

ISBN: 978 0 263 20288 5

Set in Times Roman 10¼ on 12¾ pt
07-0508-41170

Printed and bound in Great Britain
by Antony Rowe Ltd, Chippenham, Wiltshire

THE GREEK
TYCOON'S
CONVENIENT
WIFE

To all my lovely Wirdnam cousins,
especially Barbie, Christine and Jane.

CHAPTER ONE

SHE heard a car door slam, the crunch of gravel on the drive, and Alice tensed as the doorbell rang, sounding unnaturally loud as it echoed through the large house.

He was here.

Drawing a deep breath, she applied one final brush-stroke of Racy Red lipstick and then stepped back to survey her handiwork as a very different Alice stared back at her from the mirror.

Had fate stepped in to provide her with the kind of armour she suspected she might need to cope with seeing Kyros again? Normally, she would never have been wearing black satin—a dress so exquisitely fitted that it looked as if she had been poured into it. Nor silk stockings and a pair of killer heels, with their distinctive scarlet soles. The waterfall of glittering stones which dangled from her ears and lay clustered at her throat were not real, but at least they served a pur-pose—for surely their dazzle would distract her ex-lover from looking too closely into her eyes and seeing her troubled thoughts.

She wanted him to look at her and think: *Alice looks wonderful,* and she wanted him to look at her and think: *What a fool I was to let her go.* Wasn't that what every woman would want in the same situation? That a man who had walked away from their love affair so carelessly because she *wasn't Greek* should feel a pang of regret?

The doorbell rang again.

'I've only just got out of the bath!' yelled Kirsty from along the corridor, and Alice drew another breath. *Please give me strength,* she prayed as she went to answer it.

'All right!' she called. 'I'm coming!'

Her progress downstairs in the too-high heels was slow but her heart was beating like a piston as she pulled open the front door and dazzling summer light flooded in to create an unmistakable silhouette of the man who was standing there. Alice's mouth dried. Her thoughts had been spinning round and round ever since his phone call. She had tried to imagine what he might look like now—but nothing could have prepared her for the heart-stopping reality of seeing Kyros Pavlidis for the first time in ten years.

He stood in the doorway, almost filling it with his powerful frame. Black jeans and a black T-shirt moulded his hard body—the lean torso and the long, muscular legs.

Against the light she couldn't see his expression—not at first—only the glitter in his jet-dark eyes. But as she became accustomed to the brightness every feature was revealed to her. The high slash of cheekbones, the aquiline nose—and the slightly forbidding mouth which so rarely softened. His face was as hard and as formidable as she remembered—but he was still devastatingly handsome.

She gripped the heavy oak of the door, afraid that she might crumple. Or show him that she still thought he was the most amazing man she had ever set eyes on. But hot on the heels of confusion came pride. Because this was the man who had hurt her. She had gone to him an innocent and been left a cynic who'd stopped believing in love. *So remember that.*

'Hello, Kyros,' she said calmly.

For a moment Kyros did not respond as fury, disbelief and pure sexual hunger flooded through his veins in quick succession. His assessment of her had been rapid. No wedding ring. No man hovering curiously in the background, monitoring the mystery caller. *And the clothes of a whore!*

His lips curved in a mixture of distaste and appreciation as he ran his eyes over a black satin dress that showed far too much of those long legs which used to wrap themselves so spectacularly around his neck. It clung to the swell of her breasts and shimmered down over that perfect derriere. How could she contemplate going out wearing something which would make every man with a pulse think what he was thinking right now? How much he wanted her.

'*Kalespera,* Alice,' he said softly as desire began to coil itself deep within him. 'Did you forget to put your dress on—or are you simply moonlighting as a hooker?'

Despite the outrageous remark, it was the voice that was almost her undoing. She had heard it on the phone, but being coupled with the sight of him in the powerful and glowing flesh simply magnified its impact and Alice only just stopped her knees from buckling. That accent, she thought weakly. That sexy, incomparable Greek accent that took her straight back to a time which was strictly off limits.

'I told you I was going to a party,' she said, realising that already he was making her defend her behaviour!

'In a pair of shoes that should never be worn outside the bedroom,' he observed, his gaze flicking over the high, patent heels.

Alice gripped the door even tighter. 'Listen, Kyros—trading insults with someone you haven't seen for ten years isn't really the traditional method of greeting in England—or had you forgotten such basic things as manners?'

But Kyros barely heard her—he just continued staring at her intently, as if his vision would suddenly clear and the woman he had been expecting would reappear. The Alice he had known had been pure and innocent, her hair hanging in a flaxen curtain to her waist—not piled up on top of her head in some sophisticated creation of loops and curls that made her look as if she should be working in a casino. She would be clad in a pretty cotton frock or some swirly little skirt and T-shirt. She'd certainly never have worn a dress so obviously sexy or revealing. He would never have allowed her to.

But his eyes gleamed as he was caught in the emerald crossfire of her eyes. 'Okay, Alice—if it's convention you want, then convention you shall have.' He let his gaze drift over her, drinking in that glorious creamy flesh of hers. 'Long time no see,' he murmured sardonically. 'Isn't that what we should say after so many years?'

Alice felt shaken. His smooth fluency had always been such a foil to his very Greek buccaneering beauty—but that blatant undressing with his eyes had made her feel positively weak, and she wasn't going to *do* weak. 'I wasn't sure you'd turn up,' she said.

'But I told you I'd be passing.'

'Yes. Yes, I know you did.' He would pop in, he had said, as if she was nothing but a careless afterthought—which she supposed she was. Had he deliberately highlighted the fact that he wasn't putting himself out to come and see her? In case she got the wrong idea. He hadn't even told her he'd be coming alone. She peered over his shoulder, as if expecting to see some exotic Grecian beauty following obediently behind him, but to her utter relief there was no one there.

It wasn't exactly the warmest welcome he had ever received and Kyros raised his dark brows. In theory, he had known that she wouldn't be standing there with open arms—but he was still macho enough to be surprised at her coolness. Was she perhaps worried about her parents and their reaction to seeing him? 'Your mother and father are around?'

'No. Dad took early retirement from the business and they're having a new lease of life—they're on holiday in the Maldives!' Now why had she told him *that?*

Kyros's eyes narrowed. It surprised him to think of a man as vital as her father being retired. 'And you live here now?' he questioned. 'With your parents?'

Perhaps she was being hypersensitive—but now he was making her sound like some sad old spinster who had run home to her parents when her romantic dreams hadn't quite worked out. Alice laughed. 'No, of course I don't live here. I have an apartment in London. I've come back for this party.'

'And you're still planning on going to it?'

Her lips fell open into a disbelieving 'O.' 'You thought perhaps I'd cancel it once I knew you were coming?'

He gave a slow smile. 'Why not?'

She wanted to be outraged at his arrogance but how could she be when a tiny part of her had been tempted to do just that? Hadn't she felt an overwhelming urge to ask Kirsty to get ready at her own house—so that she'd be able to spend a little time alone with the black-eyed Greek she'd never really forgotten?

She'd told herself that it was normal to want to catch up on the lost years. That maybe it would help give her proper closure on their affair once and for all. But all that would have been a lie. There was only one reason why she wanted to spend time with Kyros— and it had nothing to do with talking and everything to do with his dark, sexual allure. 'Sorry to disappoint you,' she swallowed.

There was a pause. 'Ah, but you never did disappoint me, Alice,' he said softly. 'Not then, and certainly not now—despite the showgirl appearance.'

He let his eyes drift over her and suddenly Alice wondered why the hell she hadn't thrown on a silk kimono over the dress. It had been a rebellious gesture to answer the door like this—one intended to demonstrate that she might be almost thirty and unmarried but her figure was as slim and her legs as toned as they had been at university. Yet all it was managing to do was to make her feel vulnerable...naked beneath that candid appraisal which had followed on so quickly from his obvious initial disapproval.

But she couldn't turn him away, not now. Not only would it make her look foolish, it would hint to Kyros that he still exerted some kind of power over her—and he didn't, did he? Not anymore. And besides, Alice was curious. You didn't spend years wondering and aching to know what had happened to the one man you'd ever loved, only to shut the door in his face.

So wasn't this her opportunity to change the tape? To wipe the bad memories clean and replace them with new ones? To realise that Kyros was just a man and not a god, and that she had moved on. Wouldn't it be wonderful if she could do all that?

She stepped back. 'You'd better come in,' she said.

'At last,' he murmured sardonically, and as he stepped into the house it felt like a kind of victory— as he looked around the large hallway which itself was as big as a room.

It was a cosy, English family home—with its books and cushions, its walls studded with paintings and photos and its scruffy, overstuffed sofa. He remembered the first time he had come here and how alien it had seemed—for he recalled envying such an environment, while feeling stifled by it at the same time.

He remembered the home-made cake which her mother had produced. The cups of faintly scented tea in cups so delicate that they were almost transparent. And the dog which had sat at his feet—its liquid brown eyes huge as it silently begged for food.

'But you mustn't give him any,' Alice had giggled. 'He's a greedy pig!'

He had fed the dog, of course—as he suspected he had been supposed to all along, for everyone had laughed. Was that some kind of silent test he had passed? he wondered. Some crude initiation test to see whether the dark and macho Greek would be accepted into a family home which was light years away from the dysfunction of his own? For Alice had looked deep into his eyes and smiled and in that moment he had felt…

What?

Danger?

Oh, yes. Along with the certainty that he was getting in too deep—and the even greater certainty that he was much too young to settle down, and when he did it would never be with someone like Alice.

He stared at her now. Beneath the too-heavy make-up she still had the most beautiful pair of eyes he had ever seen on a woman—green and deep as a forest glade. He remembered the flow of her hair like a bright cascade—a waterfall of moonlight over her bare back. He felt the call of forgotten poetry and the hard stir to his groin and he sank down onto one of the battered sofas before it became a talking point.

'So…what exactly are you doing in England?' questioned Alice, quickly walking across to the other side of the room and away from his dangerous proximity.

He stretched his long legs out in front of him and watched with a curl of wry amusement as Alice perched herself self-consciously on a piece of furniture as far away from him as it was possible to be. That flash of bare thigh above her stocking top was quite something. 'I've been to a wedding,' he drawled.

It was the last thing she had expected him to say. Alice's fingernails gripped the sofa. Kyros and weddings went as well together as water and electricity. And didn't the very word sound uncomfortably intimate, especially to her, who had once—mistakenly as it turned out—rather hoped to marry *him?* What an idiot she had been. She stared at him. 'Anyone I know?'

'My twin brother Xandros.'

'Xandros?'

'You sound surprised.'

Alice shook her head in disbelief. 'Surprise doesn't come close to it. I thought your brother was a commitment-phobe—legendary for the number of lovers he had.'

'So he was,' he agreed, with a careless shrug. 'But it seems that even the world's most restless lovers can be tamed—for now he has met and married a woman called Rebecca—'

'She's not Greek?' Alice interrupted quickly, with a sudden painful pounding of her heart.

'No. She is English.' Their eyes met. 'Just like you.'

No, not like me at all, thought Alice trying not to allow the hurt to show. Kyros had done his best to convince her that their upbringings were too dissimilar for the relationship to work—and that the cultural differences would sound a death-knell to a shared future. Or maybe that had just been him alighting on the perfect excuse to finish a youthful romance that she'd had no desire to let go of. 'I thought that you and your brother were estranged. That you didn't speak anymore.'

Kyros raked a hand through his thick dark hair. It was true—he and Xandros had fought all their lives and eventually they had fallen out in dramatic style. His twin had left the island for America and had never returned, both brothers telling themselves it was for the best—and that was how the rift had been born. How black and white things could seem when you were eighteen years old—and then somehow life turned them grey and indistinct.

'That was a long time ago,' he said offhandedly. 'Time heals—and both of us seem to have forgotten what the original row was about. So I thought, why not go to his wedding?' It had meant a lot to Xandros, or so he had told him just before the ceremony, when he'd clasped Kyros in a fierce hug. His wincing face hidden from view, Kyros had submitted to this unheard of and unwanted display of emotion, telling himself that his brother was clearly overwrought with wedding plans.

'And is he….happy?' questioned Alice.

'Happy?' Kyros's mouth hardened. How foolish and predictable women could be—with their naïve supposition that happiness was a permanent state! Something which came ready-made and indestructible with the marriage certificate. Happiness was like a bubble—perfection itself until it popped and then it was gone, leaving no trace other than a faint memory.

Yet, undeniably, he had been slightly taken aback to observe his brother in the throes of a love affair. To see his tough twin unashamed of showing the world— and a woman—how much he adored her had filled Kyros with unease. It could not last—it rarely did— and such a weakness would come back to haunt him. As well as effectively slicing off a huge piece of his considerable fortune if they divorced.

'Oh, everyone can be happy for a while,' he said, his black eyes hardening into shards of jet as he looked at her. 'Whether it will last, who knows? I doubt it.'

'What a cynic you are,' Alice observed wryly.

'Or realist?'

Their eyes met in a long, unspoken moment until Kyros finally broke it—because the slow flicker of desire was threatening to catch fire. Her fingers were bare, yet he wanted to make sure—because the new breed of women in Western society often seemed to decline to wear a wedding band.

'You don't have a husband yourself, Alice?'

She shook her head. 'No, I don't.'

'A boyfriend, then?'

'Again, no.'

He smiled. 'No one who could match up to me, *ne?*'

Had he read her mind? Damn him. That no man had ever captured her heart and her body in the way that Kyros had. 'Certainly not in the ego department,' she said drily.

He laughed, shifting his position on the sofa very slightly. 'Nor any other department, I imagine,' he murmured.

'I really haven't given it a lot of thought,' she said, ignoring the blatantly sexual boast and praying that the lie would not show and that nothing in her expression would alert him to the sleepless nights she'd spent aching for him after he'd gone. It had taken a lot of time and a lot of work to reach a place where the thought of Kyros didn't bring an involuntary catch to her throat—and she wasn't going to throw it all away now. 'Or rather, I haven't given *you* a lot of thought.'

'Really?' he questioned sardonically.

'The past is a place I don't choose to visit often, Kyros—apparently it's best left behind,' she continued, though inside she was wondering how she could have forgotten his arrogance. His obvious belief that his memory should burn as bright as some eternal light. 'We had an affair when we were both young. It ended. So what?' She shrugged. 'It happens to everyone.'

Kyros's eyes narrowed first with disbelief, and then irritation. Was it possible that she was speaking the truth? That she could dismiss her 'affair' with him as if he were just some insipid ex-boyfriend?

Well, either she meant what she said, or she was trying to make a point—to show him she no longer cared. And either way she would take those words back, Kyros thought as the hard beat of desire made him want to take her there and then.

He had come here tonight on an impetuous and half-formed wish to see what had happened to her—but her throw-away remark was like hurling a bucket of petrol over the smouldering embers of a fire which had never quite died.

He wanted her.

Still wanted her.

And tonight he would have her. He would peel that tarty-looking dress from her body and bare the breasts he knew so well and he would take them into his mouth and suckle them. He would soon discover for himself how time had changed and refined the curves of her body and her secret feminine places.

His mouth dried. He would make her keep her shoes on. He would make love to her and finally slake his desire for her. Only this time he would walk away and he would finally be free—for there would be no lingering trace of her left in his mind or his body. He would shake off every last trace of her in one long and delicious night of sex.

'Indeed, it does happen to everyone—for nobody's experience is unique,' he agreed softly, his gaze settling on the scarlet gleam of her lips. Like a snake uncoiling itself, he rose from the sofa with a fluid grace and began to walk across the room towards her. 'So tell me about this party you're going to tonight.'

Alice's breathing began to quicken. 'There's... nothing much to tell.'

He thought of what a stir she would create in that

outrageous outfit. He thought of all the times she had dressed for him. And undressed for him, and suddenly a great rush of jealousy washed over him—hot poison firing his blood. 'Whose party is it?'

She registered the sudden animosity in his body language. 'Kyros! You can't just waltz back into my life after ten years and start interrogating me about who I associate with!'

'Can't I?' He took a step closer. 'And that still doesn't answer my question, Alice.'

He was close enough now for her to be able to detect his raw, masculine heat—the shimmering aura of sexuality which always seemed to radiate from his powerful frame. For the first time she noticed the tiny lines which fanned out from the sides of the black eyes. The faint hint of silver at the sides of his thick ebony hair. The deepening of lines around the strong, firm mouth. 'But I don't have to answer your question.'

'Whose party is it?' he persisted softly, but at that moment there was the clip-clopping of heels on the stairs and a woman wearing a very tight silver catsuit walked into the room.

'I can't breathe in this thing!' she was saying, holding a half-drunk glass of wine and smiling until she saw him, and then she stood stock-still, her face freezing like a cartoon character.

Kyros stared at her in utter disbelief. 'Who the hell is this?' he said.

Alice watched as Kirsty began to blink rapidly, as if she couldn't quite believe what she was seeing—completely ignoring the fact that his greeting had been so rude and unwelcoming. It might have been comical if it hadn't still inexplicably had the power to hurt—the sight of her best friend staring open-mouthed at Kyros as if some kind of god had just materialised.

'Well, hel-*lo,*' said Kirsty. 'You must be—'

'This is Kyros. Kyros, this is Kirsty,' said Alice quickly. 'You remember, I told you—Kyros and I knew each other at university.'

'Er, that's right,' said Kirsty, her fingers unconsciously moving up to pat at her red hair. 'But I had no idea that—'

That he was quite so stunning? Or that he was standing there in her parents' sitting room—legs apart and hands resting arrogantly on his narrow hips as if he owned the place—looking at the two of them as if a couple of aliens had just landed?

'Do you always go out dressed like this?' he demanded.

Kirsty giggled. 'Of course not—but the theme of the party is "Divine Decadence". Didn't Alice tell you?'

Black eyes fixed on Alice, sending several conflicting messages sparking at her from their ebony depths. 'No,' he said softly. 'She omitted to mention that fact. I think she found it slightly amusing to allow me to carry on thinking that she enjoyed dressing like a lady of the night, didn't you, Alice?'

'I think I did,' Alice agreed blandly, and smiled. 'Kyros was just passing by on his way back from a wedding,' she told Kirsty. 'And he's just leaving.'

'Oh!' Kirsty pouted. 'What a pity.'

Kyros's expression was lazy and complicit as he subjected the redhead to a slow smile. 'Indeed it is— for I am rarely in this country.'

Alice saw the question coming from a mile off, but it was too late to field it because Kirsty was already asking it.

'Well, why don't you come, too?'

'He can't. It's a themed party, remember?' Alice snapped. 'And Kyros isn't dressed for it!'

'Oh, I don't know—he looks divinely decadent to me,' gurgled Kirsty.

'You think so?' Kyros's lips curved into a smile. 'Well, I should like to come along if you are sure I will not be in the way? If you are sure that your host will not object, *ne?*'

He was peppering his words with Greek *deliber-ately,* thought Alice furiously, knowing damned well the effect they had on women—for hadn't they once had that same effect on her? Just as he was dazzling Kirsty with one of his rare and brilliant smiles. Either way, her friend was shaking her head as if he had just suggested the most outlandish thing on earth.

'Object—to *you?*' Kirsty gave him a conspiratorial

grin. 'I don't imagine you ever have much trouble getting into parties, Kyros! Anyway, it's a pretty casual do. The more the merrier—and single men are always at a premium.'

Especially men like you, her eyes seemed to say and Alice bit her lip, furious now. Kirsty was managing to make them sound like a small pack of man-eating women! The kind who were pushing thirty and were desperate to get their hands on anything with testosterone. How *could* she?

It was true that she had convincingly told her friend that she'd got over Kyros years ago. But she'd mainly been getting in practice for when she came face-to-face with him herself. Surely Kirsty could have guessed that she didn't want him anywhere near her?

But at least the party was local—a few short streets away. It would be all too easy to leave unnoticed once it got going—and she could lose herself in the crowd. Why, doubtless Kyros would quickly be surrounded by women and probably wouldn't even notice her slip away.

'Yes, you're very welcome to join us, Kyros,' Alice agreed indifferently, although her fast-pounding heart told a different story entirely.

Kyros felt the flare of desire mingled with curiosity as she deliberately turned away from him and he observed the stiff set of her back, which was at such odds with the delicious curve of her bottom. Was she really as immune to him as she appeared? Would he have to work very hard to get her into bed tonight?

But the prospect of such a sexual conquest as this thrilled him and it was a long time since a challenge had filled him with quite so much excitement.

CHAPTER TWO

THE party was in a big, old house whose garden spilled down to the river—and clearly no expense had been spared. It was already in full swing when they arrived, as waitresses wearing very little bobbed around with trays of exotic-looking cocktails. Fairy lights were threaded into the branches of the trees, giant torches flared on either side of a specially constructed walkway, and there was a huge marquee with loud music blasting from it.

'I'm surprised the neighbours haven't complained about the noise,' said Alice as they stood at the edge of the marquee's black and white dance floor and watched people dancing around with varying degrees of skill.

'That's because they've *invited* all the neighbours!' giggled Kirsty. 'Oh, look—there's Giles—won't be a minute, I *must* say hello!'

Alice could have screamed as she watched Kirsty wiggling her silver bottom before being swallowed up by the crowd. She might have objected to the way that her friend had been fawning over Kyros all the way over here, but the last thing she wanted was to be left alone with him.

Yet she *wasn't* alone, she reminded herself—there must be over a hundred people here with more arriving by the minute—and what could possibly happen in full view of everyone, if she didn't want it to?

'Some party,' murmured Kyros, looking around.

'Yes.' Alice saw someone she'd been at school with, and waved. 'The couple holding it are both bankers—they've just bought this house and this is their house-warming. Let's go and find them,' she suggested.

He turned then, a flicker of irritation flaring in the depths of the ebony eyes. 'But I don't want to find anyone.'

'Don't you think that's a little rude, Kyros?'

'Not really.' His mouth curved into a half-smile—the kind that usually warned people that it was point-less to waste their time arguing with him. 'Look around—see for yourself. People are drinking enough to ensure they have headaches by midnight and the more adventurous have already started dancing. In other words, Alice, everyone is doing their own thing. No one knows me—and why should they want to?'

Alice grabbed a vicious-looking purple cocktail from a passing tray and drank a potent mouthful. 'Oh, please don't be disingenuous, Kyros. Despite the fact that you're woefully underdressed compared to everyone else, every woman in the garden noticed you walking in and every man is watching you out of the corner of their eyes to see what you'll do next. Or rather, where're you'll strike.'

'Strike?' he echoed.

'Like a predator,' she said, before she had time to think about the wisdom of her words.

'Then let me put their minds at rest,' he said softly, cupping her elbow within the palm of his hand. 'I am not interested in any of the women here—except the one whose perfume is invading my senses. Is it rose?' he questioned.

'Jasmine,' she said automatically as the cocktail fizzed its way round her bloodstream.

'Ah, jasmine. Sweet and intoxicating.' Just like her. His thumb began to idly stroke at the satin texture of her skin and he felt it prickle into goose-bumps beneath his touch. 'What I want is a few uninterrupted moments alone with you—catching up as ex-lovers do. To see what the world has done to us both in the intervening years.'

'I don't think—'

'Then don't think,' he drawled dismissively. 'You're curious. I'm curious.' The pad of his thumb now traced a featherlight line down to her wrist where he could feel the thready flicker of her pulse and see the dark blue tracery of veins beneath the fair skin. 'Very curious.'

Had he deliberately couched his words to sound

like a sexual invitation? Probably. She wanted to tell him to stop touching her—just as she wanted to tell him to stop dipping his voice like that, so that it resembled rich, creamy chocolate which was gliding sweetly over her skin. But no words came—all that came was a terrible awareness of the aching emptiness inside her.

But maybe in a way, he was right. Maybe she needed to fill in the yawning gaps of her imagination with a few facts because he must have left scores of broken-hearted women behind. Women just like her. And wouldn't it be good for her to hear that? To understand that what she had shared with him had not been unique or special. It might be painful—but if she could see their relationship as it really was, rather than what she had wanted it to be, then mightn't that help take Kyros off the pedestal where he stubbornly seemed to stay, no matter how fervent her efforts to remove him?

'Okay. Why not?' she questioned carelessly, but quickly moved away from the temptation of his touch before beginning to walk away from the marquee.

The garden was long and they stopped by a quiet, shaded spot near to where the dark river water lapped against the bank—far away enough not to be bothered by stray guests or the insistent music, but Alice found that she was trembling, even though the summer air was thick and warm and scented with flowers.

He gestured to a bench which curled all the way round the trunk of a tree. 'Let's sit here.'

Though hard, the seat was oddly intimate and Alice was uncomfortably aware of how close his thigh lay to hers—and how she had to keep surreptitiously tugging at the hem of her satin dress to stop her stocking tops from showing.

'Oh, don't worry about it,' he said lazily. 'I have no objection to looking at your legs.'

'Well, I do,' she said, when he plucked the cocktail glass from her suddenly boneless fingers and put it on the grass nearby.

'You don't need that,' he said flatly.

'Says who?'

His mouth curved into a mocking smile. 'I do.'

The gesture was both autocratic and yet thrilling—and Alice was appalled at herself for thinking so. Was it because he was Greek that he seemed so utterly masculine and in total command of the situation? That he could get away with the kind of domination she wouldn't dream of tolerating from any other man—or was it simply because he was Kyros?

'As high-handed as ever, I see,' she observed.

'Ah, but women like a man to take control.' In the fading light, his eyes gleamed. 'You always did,' he added deliberately.

Especially in bed. The unspoken words seemed to filter their way through the gathering gloom towards her, pulling her back to a time of erotic awakening at Kyros's hands.

When they'd met she had been a virgin—something which had delighted him. A woman's virtue was the most precious gift that she could give to a man, he had assured her as he had removed the underwear from her trembling body with the dexterity of a man who had done so many times before.

With a passion which had dazed her, he had taught her everything he knew—and it seemed that his knowledge on this particular subject was encyclopaedic. Kyros was an expert in the art of love-making, 'Because it *is* an art, *agape mou,*' she recalled him murmuring as he had pulled her down onto his lap. How jealous she had been of all the women who had come before her— the women he had practised his art on. And what of the ones who had followed—what of those?

She wasn't going to go there. They weren't here to talk about intimacy—because that would only highlight unwanted emotions like envy and regret. Once again, she smoothed the hem of her dress.

'I thought we'd already decided it was a little late in the day for fake modesty?' he murmured.

'Fake modesty will go once you ditch the caveman comments,' she said, and he laughed. 'So let's have this catch-up you're so keen on, Kyros. What exactly are you doing these days? Where are you living?'

'On Kalfera. Where else?'

Alice had only ever seen photos of the stunning island where he and his twin brother had grown up and to her unworldly eyes it had looked like some kind of faraway paradise—with its sapphire seas and blazing white sands. Kyros had always spoken of returning there, but somehow she had thought that it might feel claustrophobic after London. She had thought that he might want to be free of its bitter memories. For hadn't he once told her—on the one and only time she'd ever seen him slightly drunk—of the mother who had walked out on him and his twin brother when they were barely four years old?

And she remembered tentatively bringing up the subject another time—and the way he had shot her down in flames, telling her never to mention it again.

She watched him now—the shadows which caressed his sculpted cheekbones. 'I thought you might find island life too small and insular—after all the freedom you enjoyed while you were studying.'

'I choose to live on an island—that doesn't mean I'm marooned on it,' he said sarcastically. 'I can move between the mainland and rest of Europe whenever it suits me.'

'And how often is that?'

'That depends. I have business interests which I'm growing, but Kalfera is where I most like to be. Life is very simple there—with a peace like nowhere else on earth. There's nowhere like it,' he finished softly, but then narrowed his eyes, shuttering them against further intrusion. So she still had that inquisitive way with her—and he had not brought her down here to this secluded spot for Alice to be interrogating him about his choice of home!

'But that is enough about my unsophisticated life on a little Greek island,' he murmured, leaning back against the tree trunk so that he could study the slim swell of her breasts. 'I want to hear all about you.'

It occurred to Alice that he had actually told her very little about himself, other than where he was living. Had he made a success of the family business, she wondered—because hadn't the company been struggling at some point? she recalled. Her eyes flicked over his jeans and T-shirt—not exactly the outfit of a rich man. Was it struggling still—and did that explain his reluctance to talk about it?

'Oh, I've done okay,' she said quietly. She didn't want to boast—particularly if Kyros hadn't made the dizzy and expected rise to the top—but neither did she want to play down her achievements. Even if her love life hadn't been a success, at least Alice's job was the one constant area she could be relatively proud of. 'Enough to be able to support myself, anyway—and to own my own apartment.'

How long would it take to drive there? he wondered idly. In time for bed? 'Doing what?'

'I'm in marketing.' She thought she saw his mouth curve and stupidly found herself rushing to her own defence! 'It may sound a little dull, but it's anything but—especially in the company I've joined. We sell health-care products—alternative therapy stuff—which is big business now. When I started out, things were on a downward spin—but we rethought our marketing strategies and it coincided with a change in people's thinking, and…' she shrugged, suddenly aware of the gleam in his black eyes '…now it's on the upturn.'

'Ah, Alice—how passionately you speak of this *business*. So you have become a career woman?' he observed mockingly.

'You make it sound like a fault.'

'Do I? That is too strong an assessment—though nobody can deny that it is different for a woman. That if she puts her heart into her career, it leaves little room for anything else,' he mused, glancing down at her bare fingers. 'Particularly a family.'

Don't take it personally, she told herself, but the taste of regret made her bite her lip. *Just because you've never settled down and had children doesn't mean you're any kind of failure,* she told herself firmly. 'There's still plenty of time for that,' she returned, horribly aware that she might now be sounding even more defensive.

'You think that women can have it all?' he questioned.

'I think men would like them to believe they can't—but that they owe it to themselves to try.'

'So you have become the arch-feminist in your silk stockings and suspenders,' he observed drily, aware of the sudden kick of lust.

Now his black gaze was sliding down over her body, making her skin tingle with a growing kind of awareness. 'I don't remember you being quite so out-rageously old-fashioned—even in the past,' she returned. 'Did you turn the clock back by a century when you returned to Kalfera?'

He stretched out his long legs in front of him and he saw her shift a little, as if her own position was uncomfortable. Was it? Well, it was pretty uncomfortable for *him*—but maybe that was because the inexorable build-up of desire was pulling tight across the heavy denim of his jeans. Would she notice? he wondered. What would she do if he put her hand there? Would she stroke him and then unzip him and take him into her mouth as she had done so many times in the past?

'So have you missed me, *agape mou?*' he murmured, cursing himself against the now exquisitely painful ache.

It was a long time since she had heard that particular term of affection—it was one of the first and few Greek phrases she had learned and now it took her by surprise. But more crucially, it took her back to a time and a place which she had sectioned off as being too dangerous—rather as you might wire-fence a crater you'd found lurking at the bottom of your garden.

Forgetting Kyros had been something she'd taught herself to do after he'd gone. It hadn't been easy—but time had helped and so had practice. Yet seeing him here like this hurtled her back to a forgotten time and suddenly she found she had no defence against the flood of memories which washed over her.

They had met during her first month at college—
at a party thrown to welcome the 'freshers'. She had
been eighteen and bright and eager to learn about
anything life could throw at her and Kyros had been
the pin-up Greek who was just starting his final year.
Everyone had known Kyros—and he had been more
exotic than anyone she'd ever met in the small town
where she'd grown up.

His glowing olive skin, black hair and hard tall
body were the dream package. And so too were his arrogance and unashamedly macho attitude. At a time
when Englishmen had been trying to get in touch with
their feelings, Kyros had been their dark antithesis
and women had clustered around him like flies.

Alice remembered feeling slightly appalled at how
obvious some of those women could be and he was
rumoured to have slept with at least three of them. But
she hadn't paid him any attention—not because of
some kind of sophisticated game-plan, because she
hadn't had the experience to play games. No, she had
simply looked at him and decided that he was way out
of her league, her experience, her world—everything,
really.

Years later she would understand that men like
Kyros were natural predators—that they liked the
chase and they liked the new. It had been her fresh-
ness and innocence and her lack of interest in him
which had drawn him to her—just as nature had pro-
grammed her to respond to his alpha qualities.

Physical attraction was one thing but Alice had fallen in love with him because, well, because he was Kyros and she couldn't not have loved him. And for a time he had loved her too—or so he'd said. But love had not prevented him from walking away from her as clinically as he had. Leaving with a regretful shrug, which had done nothing to dull the pain of his words.

But you must have known I would return to take over the family business, agape mou. *In time I shall no doubt marry a beautiful Greek girl who will produce at least five children—most of whom will be sons! And they in turn will take over the business from me one day. That is the way these things work.*

No, she had not known at all—or rather, had not allowed herself. She had wanted their relationship to endure and she had cried—but at least she had stopped short of begging him not to go.

And once Alice had seen that his mind was made up, she had forced herself to allow herself a glimpse of her own future. And despite her heartache, she had allowed herself the first faint flare of hope. Soon she would have a degree with which to launch her career. She might no longer have Kyros, she had reasoned— but out there lay travel and fun and excitement for her to sample.

That her life had not materialised according to her dreams was nobody's fault—let alone Kyros's.

The memories cleared and Alice saw his ebony eyes gleaming in the moonlight as the music from the party drifted down the garden towards them. She swallowed. What had his question been? The one which had set off all those bitter-sweet thoughts about the past? Had she missed him? he had asked—with all the sensitivity of a steamroller. How could a man be so dense? In the beginning, she had missed him with the agony of someone who'd had one of their limbs cut off!

But worse than missing him had been the realisation that never again would she meet a man who came anywhere close to Kyros Pavlidis and the way he made her feel. She remembered understanding that with a painful kind of clarity and she had been proved absolutely right.

She would never tell him *that,* of course—his ego did not need such a boost—but neither could she deny having missed him at all, for surely it was impossible to tell an outright lie of that magnitude? It would make her sound like a fraud.

But she could choose how to tell him, for she was no longer a young, impressionable girl rocked by the urgent power of first love.

'It was inevitable that I should miss you to some extent,' she said. 'We'd been an item for nearly a year. It went from full time to nothing.' Still warmed by the cocktail, she even managed a fairly convincing smile. 'I suppose what I found odd was the abruptness of it all. You never wrote, or phoned. You disappeared completely from my life. I never saw you or heard from you again.' So that sometimes it had seemed like some strange and glorious dream.

His mouth curved into a hard, mocking line. 'It was better that way,' he said. 'If we'd stayed friends…' What? He might have been tempted to come back and to take her to bed and lose himself in her body over and over again? He had wanted—no, needed—to make a clean break with her. To forget his blonde lover—with her long legs and her emerald eyes.

But he had never forgotten her, he realised that now. Nor got her completely out of his system. He had buried his hunger for Alice—and he was only just discovering how deeply. And now? Just like a seed which had lain dormant all these years and been suddenly fed light and air and water, his desire for her was fizzing over like a warm glass of champagne, given life by the sight of her sitting like some goddess in the moonlight, her hair a silvery fall down her back.

'We could never have stayed friends, Alice,' he said harshly. 'Ex-lovers don't make good friends.'

'No,' she said, forcing a smile. 'I guess you're right.'

Her green eyes were unreadable in the dim light. He had expected—what? That she, of all people—having tasted the pleasures of his body—would respond to him as other women did? That she would be pouting and sending out silent signals that she wanted him? But Alice had not done that.

It was true that she was dressed like a siren—but

she had not followed that up with any suggestiveness. And hadn't that always been part of her attraction to him? Her cool blonde beauty hiding the rampant sensual fire beneath?

So what was he going to do about it? He was going to do what he always did—take what he wanted, and then walk away.

Reaching out his hand, he splayed his fingers over the base of her throat—just below the necklet of fake gemstones. He could feel her pulse skittering beneath the delicate skin, could see the way that her lips parted instinctively. In the fading light her eyes darkened.

'Kyros…'

He pulled her into his arms and stared down at her, his features tense and black eyes bright with sexual hunger as they roved over her face. Alice knew in that moment that he was going to kiss her and that it would have been easier to have floated down to the end of the garden than to have resisted him. He knew that and she knew that. 'You bastard,' she whispered.

His laugh was soft as he trickled a careless finger over the pert bud of her satin-covered nipple and it tightened in response. 'But you like that. You like your hard, tough, Greek macho man, don't you, my beauty? It turns you on. It always did.'

'Kyros—' But any protest was lost then for he was crushing his lips down on hers and she was kissing him back as if her life depended on it.

Her fingers fluttered up as they sought the broad

shoulders, pressing against the hard muscle and wanting to tear away the T-shirt and to touch the silk of the olive skin beneath. She sucked in a breath—his breath—and moaned his name into his mouth.

With an angry kind of curse he pulled her down from the bench onto a soft patch of grass and pressed his body hard into hers. He felt so…so…hard. But that was okay, Alice thought weakly—because at least it was honest. She didn't want softness—she didn't want anything that masqueraded as love. This was what her hungry body craved—this virile man who was kissing her more passionately than any other man could.

Locking her arms tight around him, she kissed him back with a wantonness which felt as if it had been building up since last time he had kissed her all those years ago.

'Alice!' He let out a groan as she wriggled beneath him—the touch of her so shockingly and instantly familiar, but this time tempered with the spice of absence. His mouth at her throat, he nudged his thigh insistently against hers and they opened for him immediately and Kyros groaned with a kind of stunned disbelief. Her desire was simple and straightforward. She would play no games. She never had. Her sexual appetite had been more than a match for his—had he somehow thought that time might change that?

Heart pounding like a piston in his chest, he skated his hand down the front of her dress—the siren call of her body urging him on as he rucked up the slippery fabric of her dress, stroking his hand along the cool silk of her thigh until it alighted on her panties, and then he slipped his finger inside her.

At that she gasped, her eyes snapping open, and even in the shadow of the evening he could see they were dense and black with desire just as he could feel her barely contained shiver of delight.

'Kyros! Stop it. We…we can't—'

His hand stilled. Alice—*refusing* him?

'We can't…stay here.'

In the moonlight he smiled as he moved against her heated flesh. 'No?'

Alice groaned—her hungry body calling out to her—but some last shred of sanity made her shake her head. Because how the hell would it look if someone found them locked in an intimate embrace? Did she think so little of herself that she could allow such an easy seduction? 'No,' she moaned. 'There are people at the other end of the garden.'

In the darkness, his mouth curved into a hard smile. That did not sound like a refusal—more like a delaying tactic. He eased back from her a little, recognising the need to quieten down his aroused body or there was the very real fear that he would be unable to walk.

He stood up, and held his hand out to her. 'Get up,' he demanded unevenly. 'We're going back to your house.'

Alice steadied her ragged breathing. 'But…what will people think?'

'I don't care what people think, Alice.'

Warning bells went off in her head at his arrogant statement, reminding her that she was risking getting hurt all over again.

'Well, I do,' she said.

'Not enough to stop me,' he taunted softly, his hands now cupping her silky bottom and bringing her hard up against the cradle of his desire. 'Is it enough to stop you, Alice?'

Say no. Say it's wrong. Too soon. That any respect he may have had for you will be destroyed by this ill-advised passion. Say no!

'No,' she admitted tremblingly as she imagined him deep inside her.

He caught her fingers in his and began moving purposefully down the garden. Alice could hear chatter and music, the tinkling of crockery on china, and little shrieks of laughter as they passed. How perfectly *normal* it all sounded, she thought—with a sudden pang. While she was sneaking away like a thief in the night with a man who had already hurt her.

Was she crazy? Yes, very probably. But by now they had slipped unnoticed out of the side gate and she found herself wondering whether he made a habit of this as he led her confidently through the streets—as if *she* were the stranger in her home town.

They walked in a breathless kind of silence and when they reached her parents' house, he tipped her face up. 'Is your friend due to sleep over here tonight?'

She shook her head.

'Good.'

How clinical he was, she thought—and how well thought out his line of questioning as he took all the known factors into account, a bit like some hot-shot lawyer. But Alice could guess at his overriding concern. That he didn't want to wait and didn't want to be disturbed. The tautness in his hard body was as tight as a stretched bow and the crackling tension between them was almost palpable.

He drifted his fingertips along her cheek—as if he was using the power of touch to dissolve any last, lingering doubts. And, oh, didn't it work a treat? But Alice was past caring whether the gesture had been cynically manipulative or not. To be honest, she was past caring about anything except how much she ached to be in his arms and his bed once more.

'K-Kyros,' she said shakily, her tongue snaking out to moisten her parchment-dry lips.

'Let's get inside,' he said roughly.

CHAPTER THREE

ONCE inside, Kyros took command—turning to where Alice stood in the shadows of the hall, the ticking of the grandfather clock muffled by the loud thunder of her heart. And then he said something low and harsh in Greek, and pulled her into his arms—and suddenly this was serious.

His lips were hard, expert, seeking—and Alice swayed with the great tide of emotion which was rising up inside her as she kissed him back with a passion which seemed to have been on hold for the last ten years—and how sad was that? But Alice didn't care. The urgent touch of his lips felt so right. His body seemed to fit so perfectly as it moulded against hers. His hands slid the black satin dress up over her bottom, moving luxuriously over the lace of her panties, and as she gave a little cry he suddenly drew back, staring down into her widened eyes.

'If we don't move from here, I'm going to rip this

dress off and do it to you right here on the floor of this hall,' he ground out.

The graphic words startled her. These were no sweet nothings he was murmuring, she realised— more a cold-blooded declaration of sexual intent. But his hands were undoing all the harshness of his words, making her shiver with desire as his fingers collided with bare flesh.

'Is that what you want, Alice? To do it here?'

If it had been her own place she suspected the answer would have been yes—because that would have been easier, to have let passion carry them along in its mindless blur. But it wasn't—it belonged to her parents—and what if one of the neighbours suddenly decided to call round for whatever reason? Unlikely— but terrifying. 'N-no,' she breathed. 'Not here.'

'Where?' he demanded, his mouth on hers.

'Up-upstairs.'

'Show me.'

As they climbed the stairs Alice realised that there was time to stop this madness. Even as she pushed open the door of her old bedroom—now transformed into the creamy comfort of a guest room—she knew there was still time. But the moment he had kicked the door shut and taken her into his arms again to smother her with hard, passionate kisses Alice knew it was too late.

Kyros moaned as her mouth opened beneath his and his desire shot up to an explosive level—but then she had always possessed the power to turn his blood to fire. He knew everything there was to know about a woman's body. How to make her cry with pleasure and weep with joy. How to tease and retreat—to play the sophisticated games of the bedroom, which only increased the levels of mutual delight.

But tonight all his usual finesse seemed to have deserted him and he groaned with disbelief as he slid his hand up over the cool silk of her thigh and encountered her hot, wet sweetness—so ready and waiting for him and he wanted to take her right there.

Growling an ancient curse in Greek, he unzipped the satin dress and threw it to the ground with utter contempt for its delicate fabric. 'We don't want *that!*' he bit out.

'I…I *hired* that outfit—it isn't actually….mine,' protested Alice breathlessly between kisses—feeling that somehow it was her *duty* to protest, maybe as a way of denying that it had actually thrilled her to have him discard it like that.

'Get them to bill me for another,' he growled as he stepped back to survey her—proprietorial and jealous as he wondered how many men after him had seen this woman clad only in her lingerie. 'Sweet heaven,' he groaned. 'Alice.'

Her underwear was as decadently black as the dress. 'Don't tell me you hired *these?*' he breathed as he skimmed the flat of his hand over high-cut panties, which emphasised the sinfully long legs and flawless curve of her derriere.

'N-no. Of course not.'

His fingers hooked inside a stocking top. 'And do you always wear stockings?' he demanded.

Did he arrogantly think she'd worn them just for him? 'Sometimes.'

Swamping the dark wave of jealousy which washed over him, Kyros forced himself to draw back once again from the inexplicable desire to ravish her there and then—without any kind of preliminaries. Because that was not how Kyros Pavlidis made love! Hardening his heart against the sudden quiver of her lips, he feasted his eyes instead on her flimsy attire. But something was not right.

His eyes travelled to where her hair was piled intricately on top of her head and he nodded. 'Take down your hair,' he commanded silkily.

Her fingers were trembling as first she pulled off the paste earrings and necklace and placed them in a glittering heap on a small table. Then she lifted her hand to her hair and began to pull out all the little clips, putting each one down to join the jewellery. Coil after coil of it fell free, until at last she gave a shake of her head and all the golden hair shimmered down—a pale waterfall which rippled to her waist, tumbling down over the provocative underwear.

He made a small sound in the back of his throat at the vision she made—both pure and sexy all at the same time. 'Ah, *ne,*' he breathed. *'Yes!'* And without warning, he bent and lifted her up in his arms.

'Kyros!'

'What?'

'Put me down!'

'You don't like a man to carry you to bed? Doesn't that still turn you on, Alice?'

Of course it did. Not that anyone else had ever done it. But some nagging doubt in the back of Alice's mind told her that Kyros still seemed to need to control everything, even after all this time—and surely that couldn't be right? But by then he had put her on the bed and was surveying her with a kind of proprietorial arrogance.

'Now.' His eyes glittered like jet as he yanked the T-shirt over his head.

Alice swallowed. His torso was lean, with not one ounce of spare flesh visible on its honed surface. Had she thought that he might have fleshed out a little? Well, she had been completely wrong.

His hand went to the fly of his jeans and he captured her hungry gaze with a look of mocking laughter. 'We certainly don't want these, do we, Alice?'

Aware that he was playing with her as a cat would a mouse, Alice forced herself to shrug. 'Oh, I don't know, Kyros—a pair of jeans certainly never stopped you in the past.'

Her teasing retort made him grow even harder—

unbearably hard. 'You...*witch!*' he declared softly as he unzipped himself.

'Am I?'

'Like Circe herself,' he said unevenly. He kicked away the jeans and dark, silky boxers before moving over to the bed, arrogantly assured in his nakedness, and Alice was startled by her first renewed sight of an aroused Kyros.

'Kyros.' His name slipped off her tongue.

'Do you want me?' he questioned.

More than anything else she could think of. 'C-come to bed,' she said again, only this time her voice was shaking with an emotion she did not want to identify as he took her into his arms and began to kiss her.

Not since his very first sexual experience had Kyros been so eager to lose himself inside a woman. 'Let's get rid of these, shall we?' he said unsteadily, sliding her panties down.

'Oh.'

'And this.' He unclipped her bra, taking each rosy-tipped breast into his mouth until he had her gasping with pleasure. This was going to happen so quickly, he thought—with a surge of pure desire which pierced him like an arrow. 'Now...'

She could feel the change in his body as he began to move over her.

'But...I've still got my shoes on,' she said breath-lessly.

'I know you have.' His lips curved as he flicked them a glance. 'Shoes like that are made for the bedroom and for wrapping around my back.'

Something in his eyes and in his voice made Alice shed the very last of her inhibitions.

'Only if you do it to me right now,' she whispered back.

Just in time he remembered protection, reaching for a condom from the back pocket of his jeans.

And, despite the good sense it made, Alice was unprepared for the sudden rush of disappointment at his forethought. 'Were you so certain you'd take me to bed, then, Kyros?'

What did she want him to say—that the thought had never crossed his mind? Honesty warred with diplomacy as he wished she'd chosen a better time to ask him. 'I was pretty sure that the chemistry between us would still exist, *ne.*'

'Chemistry?' Alice gave a short laugh. 'You mean like a series of reactions in a laboratory?'

'Don't over-think it, Alice,' he ground out. 'Don't spoil it with analysis. I thought we were just going to enjoy it—to take this one night and savour it.'

She didn't remember them saying *that.*

'Because if you've changed your mind, then you'd better tell me.'

One night. It was what it was—more to do with lust than love—but as she felt the warmth of his body so close to hers, Alice knew that sending him away wasn't an option. 'No, I haven't changed my mind,' she whispered.

Past and present seemed to fuse so that none of this felt quite real and Kyros gave a soft, low moan as he thrust into her as easily as a knife into warm butter, and he thought she whispered his name.

But then he couldn't think of anything—except how exquisitely sweet this felt, how making love to Alice had always been better than with any other woman. He kissed her as he sensed the change happening in her, even before he felt the tightening of her body around him and then its subtle arching—like a bow before the arrow left it. Or heard the little cries which accompanied every long, sweet spasm. Or saw the soft rose-bloom which flowered over her skin.

And by then it was happening for him, too—sooner than he had planned it to. And even though the sensation was always the closest feeling to heaven on earth Kyros felt as though this particular sensation had just catapulted him up into the stars.

Afterwards he let her go, wanting to turn away and fall asleep, to put some necessary physical distance between them, but finding it impossible.

'This bed is too damned small,' he complained.

It wasn't what Alice wanted to hear—but maybe she needed to. He wasn't lying there, like she was, in a dreamy daze—while even dreamier thoughts came rushing into her head.

Thoughts like: *That was extraordinary. The most*

wonderful thing to happen to me since he left. Or infinitely more disturbing thoughts like: *I think I still love him. Maybe I've never stopped loving him.* Because that was rubbish. Love meant much more than that. Good sex was just good sex—and it had always been dynamite with him. *That's all it was,* she told herself. But already her defences felt undermined—the intimacy of his presence beside her making her feel weak.

So just play it cool. Play it like he did. Complain about the lack of room, the way his thigh is lying across your thigh—something, anything. *Just don't let him see how dangerously vulnerable you are in this sleepy state after sex.*

'The bed *is* a little small,' she agreed, with a yawn. 'But then it *was* designed for one. There's another one over there—but if you find it too cramped, maybe you should go and find yourself a hotel room.'

Kyros narrowed his eyes. *Find yourself a hotel room?* Was she out of her mind or was she simply trying to provoke him? Shouldn't she be kissing him all over—moving her lips down his body to where he was already hard and growing harder still, and telling him, between kisses, that he was the most fantastic lover in the world? Not suggesting that he *leave* her!

Idly, he began to play with her breast, circling the deep-hued centre with his thumb so that it puckered and tightened. Then he bent his head to it, flicking his tongue there almost experimentally—as if he had never licked her breast before. He felt her tense.

'You want me to go?'

'That wasn't what I said.'

'That's what it sounded like. What do you want? This?' He stroked his hand down to her belly, tiptoeing his finger into the slight dip there, and she trembled as he skimmed it downwards, her face flushing pink as it alighted on the most sensitive part of her.

'Kyros,' she whispered as he began to move his fingers against her heated flesh.

His mind was working quickly even as he brought her towards orgasm. He hadn't planned this seduction—and it might so easily not have happened. There would have been nothing other than a coolly polite drink if she had been involved with another man.

But she was not involved. She was free and she was here—like a rich, ripe fruit which had fallen into his waiting arms. If he had written the script for what had just happened between them, he could not have improved on it. A no-strings one-night stand with Alice.

So why was he not even now putting his clothes on? Especially since she had just given him the perfect opportunity to walk away while they were both still flushed and sated with the aftermath of passion. And that way they would be spared the embarrassing goodbyes in the cold light of day.

Kyros stared down at her as she moved her hips in time to the rhythm of his finger. *Because once was not enough,* he realised. *Not nearly enough!*

He made a hasty mental calculation. She was crying out now, peaking against him, and ruthlessly he waited until she had stilled—before tracing the line of her still shivering lips with his finger.

'Can you get time off work?' he questioned roughly.

His unexpected question brought her unwillingly back to earth and her own intimately feminine scent assailed her nostrils and heightened her colour further. 'Like when?'

'How about next week?'

As she stared up into his face Alice thought that the pleasures of sex had not softened those hard features—nor made the brilliant black eyes any less enigmatic. 'But why, Kyros?'

He didn't miss a beat. 'Because my plans are flexible. I can stay on in England for a few extra days. And I find that I want to. You see, I want to continue what we've just been doing.' He gave the glittering smile of the predator. 'Wouldn't you?'

Yes, of course she would—and the finest actress in the world wouldn't have convinced him otherwise. But what about pride and what about principle? She had already behaved in a way which she wasn't sure she was going to like very much in the cold, clear light of day—if one of her friends had behaved in the same way and asked her opinion about it, wouldn't she have been doubtful, even a little bit disapproving? What must he think of her, lying here like this—

wearing nothing but silk stockings and a pair of very high-heeled shoes?

Yet Kyros's view of her was already formed—she wasn't going to change it now. But she needed to be certain exactly what he had in mind. 'You mean an affair?' she questioned.

Kyros gave a slow smile. *Affair* sounded a little long-term for what he had in mind, but at least she hadn't fallen into the self-delusional trap of calling it a relationship. That meant they both knew exactly where they stood. 'That is exactly what I mean, *agape mou*. We could even go away for a few days, if you like.'

Alice bit her lip. She could turn him down flat. Tell him that she didn't exist to jump to his every need and desire—and yet wouldn't she be hurting herself more than anyone? She was no longer the gullible innocent who worshipped the ground which Kyros walked on. Wouldn't a week of dealing with his arrogance make her count her blessings that he was nothing but a temporary fixture—good sex or not?

And what about your feelings? questioned a small voice in her head. *Wasn't your heart broken the first time you split with him—what's to say it won't be broken again?*

Alice closed her mind to the voice.

'I'll talk to my boss on Monday,' she said.

CHAPTER FOUR

ALICE slammed the suitcase shut and stared at it uneasily, trying to ignore the doubts which kept coming back to haunt her—no matter how much she tried to hold them at bay. Wondering whether she was doing the right thing by agreeing to go away with Kyros. And deep down she knew that the answer was: probably not.

They had certainly been nonplussed at the office when she'd asked if she could have a week off. Efficient Alice wasn't playing by her usual rules.

'I know it's short notice,' she had told her normally sympathetic line manager.

'Well, it is—a little. Can't it wait, Alice?'

And Alice guessed it was a measure of how badly she wanted the trip that she hadn't taken the hint and done the sensible thing of telling Kyros that it was much too last-minute for her to seriously consider it.

Instead, she had stuck to her guns, spurred on by a desire which at times seemed to overwhelm her. She had worked hard for her company, had given it her all for many years now—so surely she could have a little bit of payback? She was a flesh and blood creature, after all—not a robot! Flesh and blood...

Alice swallowed. Oh, yes. Certainly that.

She and Kyros had spent the rest of that night together—and she suspected she could have counted the amount of sleep she'd had in minutes. Between drowsy kisses the following morning she had asked him to leave and said she'd meet him in London.

'Let me drive you,' he drawled, but he was kissing the back of her neck as he spoke, his fingers inching their way up her thigh.

Alice wriggled away from him. His passion and stamina were almost as daunting as her response to him. 'Actually, I do have a car here—I wasn't antici- pating this was going to happen and that you would whisk me home,' she said drily. 'I'll drive myself back to London and you can come and pick me up at my flat—provided it's okay with work.'

'It had better be okay,' was his silky response.

Now Alice glanced at her watch, aware of the nervous skitter of her heart as she waited for him to arrive. He was late. Maybe he'd changed his mind about the whole idea after all. And wouldn't that be the best of all solutions—certainly for her?

The ringing of the doorbell shattered her muddled thoughts and Alice quickly checked the apartment. That had been another reason for wanting to come back and spend last night here alone. So that she could rearrange her surroundings to satisfy even the most critical eye.

Because just as the clothes you wore said something about the image you wanted to project to other people, so too did where you lived. This wasn't just her apartment in London which Kyros would be seeing—this was, in effect, her showing him what her life was like and what she had achieved. How hard she'd worked and how well she'd done to get on the costly London property ladder.

She looked around. She was proud of her little flat. Uncluttered and sleek, it had a stunning view over the Thames—so that the light which flooded in was amazing. Daily, she saw stunning sunsets and sunrises. She watched the boats go by and heard the shouts of laughter of people walking along the bank.

Last night had been spent cleaning and polishing— and this morning she'd rushed out to the florist's to buy long-stemmed roses. Flowers made even the smallest place look sensational—and these flowers would still look beautiful at the end of the week, when she came back.

The doorbell rang a second time, and Alice went to answer it, her mouth drying with a mixture of desire and fear when she saw him again. Because this felt peculiar—as if she were meeting Kyros for the first time instead of having had wild sex with him less than twenty-four hours ago.

'Hello,' she said, almost shyly.

Hard black eyes swept over her. He had been hoping she might launch herself straight into his arms, wearing a short skirt with no panties underneath. He certainly hadn't expected to see her standing there blushing like a born-again innocent—in a pale pair of linen trousers and a pretty but distinctly unsexy top. Just as he hadn't expected her to insist on spending last night here alone. It seemed that she was going to need a little tuition in how he liked a woman to behave. 'Ready?' he asked coolly.

Alice frowned. Surely this wasn't how the grown-up versions of themselves went about things after they'd been so intimate? Whatever happened to courtesy and respect? 'Would you like to come in for a minute?'

Kyros bit back an impatient sigh. Not really, no. For a start he didn't trust himself not to start making love to her and this time he didn't want to be on *her* territory. Not again. That night in her childhood home had unsettled him—something he had put down to the powerful pull of the past. But he guessed that there was a certain kind of *protocol* which needed to be observed during these kinds of situations and he gave a brief smile.

'Why not?' He followed her inside, almost colliding with the suitcase which dominated the hallway as he began to follow her through the apartment, more tantalised by the sway of her bottom than by the guided tour she was giving him. He gave the room a quick glance. At least this wasn't going to take very long, given its size.

'And this is a painting of a place just farther along the river from here. I bought it last year,' she was saying—pointing to a surprisingly good watercolour of a rainy-day river.

'Have you packed your passport?' he questioned suddenly.

Alice turned round from the painting. 'My passport? Why?'

'I thought we'd go to Paris.'

Paris? The city of love and romance! Despite all her good intentions, Alice's heart leapt with an eager kind of longing until she reminded herself that she was not going to give into unrealistic expectation. Even so, *Paris...*

'Paris?' she repeated, aware of the faintly breathless quality to her voice and hoping he didn't pick up on it.

He gave a half-smile. 'I have a little business that I need to attend to. It won't take long—and for the rest of the time we can enjoy the city.'

Alice hid her disappointment. So she was to be sandwiched around a business meeting! Not only that—but she had just paid out a small fortune to get the bathroom redecorated and money was tight. 'I don't know that my budget will stretch to a week in Paris,' she said truthfully.

Kyros stilled. Was she trying to insult him? 'That was not my intention. I am not proposing to ask you to contribute towards the cost of the trip, Alice,' he said coldly.

'I always pay my way.'

'I will not hear of it,' he negated flatly.

Alice remembered how proud he had been over money and how it had seemed to be at the root of a lot of the arguments between him and his twin. 'Well, I won't come if you don't let me chip in,' she said stubbornly. 'Especially if money is tight for you too.'

Kyros studied her dispassionately, wondering if this was some kind of joke. But he could see from the determined expression on her heart-shaped face that she was deadly serious. She thought that money was *tight* for him, did she? He might have laughed if she hadn't been so way off mark.

'This trip,' he said softly, 'is something I've been planning for quite a while. So I'm paying for everything—do you understand that, Alice?'

Their eyes met and clashed across the narrow hallway and the fizz of tension began to hum through the air around them.

'Do I have a choice?' she questioned unsteadily.

'I'm afraid you don't.' The black eyes glittered. 'And aren't you forgetting the most important thing? You still haven't kissed me.'

'You haven't kissed me either,' she said, but her

forthright words belied the sudden insecurity which was bubbling up inside her. This felt so…strange.

'Are you going to come here, or is this going to be another battle of wills?' he murmured.

She realised that he was laughing softly and some-how that disarmed her more than anything. But as Alice went into his waiting arms she suddenly realised that this wasn't going to be easy. She wanted him—but she didn't know how to behave, and there weren't any rules in this kind of situation. He wasn't married, so she wasn't technically a mistress—but somehow that was how it felt.

Tipping her chin upwards, he curved his mouth into a hard smile. 'Or perhaps you have learnt that the most effective aphrodisiac is to keep a man guessing?'

He brought his lips down onto hers then, effec-tively closing the subject. She felt the hard, seeking warmth of his lips and her own opening beneath them. The answering curl of heat which began to spiral up inside her. 'Kyros,' she moaned as his hand reached down to unzip her trousers.

'Mmm?'

The linen she had so carefully pressed was now fluttering to the hardwood floor and his hands were ex-ploring the globes of her bottom, covered in a pair of sheer, silk panties she'd never worn before.

She drew her mouth away from his. 'I thought you were keen to get going?'

His voice was unsteady. 'That was before you began to entice me into staying.'

'I don't remember enticing you.'

'Don't you? Don't you realise that you entice me just by existing? Just by being you?' He drifted his fingertips round to lie against her searing heat and felt her squirm as he moved them beneath the delicate fabric to find her honeyed sweetness.

'Kyros!' she gasped.

The word sounded like a slurred incitement and the fire was burning through him with a speed and an intensity which took him by surprise. He unzipped his trousers and pushed her to the ground, not caring that the wood was hard and unforgiving—for neither, it appeared, did Alice. Her hands were clutching at him, her mouth greedily kissing him as he took the panties between his hands and ripped apart the delicate fabric in a single movement.

'Kyros!' she said again.

Fractionally, he moved away to slide on a condom and then paused for one, glorious moment of anticipation before entering her with a slick, easy thrust and watching her body as it reacted to his. The automatic way she tightened around him. The way her head jerked back—so that her blonde hair shimmered behind her like a silken pillow.

'Kyros!' The muffled cry was torn from her lips as he began to move inside her—and Alice had never felt quite so decadent. For a moment she imagined herself outside her own body, looking down. Seeing herself with her linen trousers down by her ankles, her top pushed up and the tattered remains of her panties lying on the floor beside her. Seeing the dark, partially clothed body of her Greek lover as he thrust into her. Utterly fulfilling and yet emotionally empty.

But then rational thought melted in the wake of desire—hot and piercing and fierce as he took her into a place of such sweetness that it made her want to weep. She wanted to kiss him, and kiss him, and kiss him. She wanted to prolong the exquisite sensation of having Kyros deep inside her—but all too quickly she was being engulfed by waves of fulfilment so sharp and so intense that for a moment Alice felt as if she had briefly lost consciousness, until she was startled by his own, wild cry.

Afterwards she clung to him and he lifted his head to study her—her cheeks flushed, her eyelids weighted and heavy, but as they fluttered open to look up at him he saw that her emerald eyes were wary.

'You liked that?'

Her tongue snaked out to moisten bone-dry lips. 'You know I did.'

He heard the hesitation in her voice. 'But?'

If she told him that each time he took her to heaven and back with his body, he chipped away a little of her heart, wouldn't that sound at best like vulnerability— at worst like a fundamental kind of weakness? As if she were some innocent little girl instead of an independent woman who had gone into this with her eyes open.

'You've ruined the outfit I was planning to wear,' she said instead.

His mouth twisted into a parody of a smile. 'Good. I didn't particularly like it—it is much too mannish for someone as fundamentally feminine as you, *thespinis mou.*' He stroked a strand of hair away from her cheek. 'I do not want you wearing trousers in future.'

Alice met the obdurate glitter of his eyes. 'That's completely outrageous.'

'It is also true. Legs like yours are much too beautiful for trousers and they only…get in the way.' He splayed his hand possessively against the cool skin of her inner thigh. 'Don't they?'

She swallowed, shivering at his touch. He *was* outrageous, but he was also right. And in that moment Alice decided that if she was going to play the part of mistress—she would play it with aplomb. She had one week with her Greek lover and she would leave every inhibition behind. Wriggling beneath him, she saw his eyes darken. 'Then I won't wear them any more,' she whispered, mock-innocently. 'Only dresses and skirts from now on. Will that please you, Kyros?'

Kyros cursed as he felt himself hardening again— her sudden submissiveness turning him on even more. 'If you don't move away from me, then we're going to end up spending the night here, *omorfus mou,*' he said dangerously. 'And I don't intend to do that. So run along and put something on which *will* please me. We have a plane to catch.'

CHAPTER FIVE

SUNLIGHT slanted in through the shutters, casting bright, horizontal stripes of light across the rumpled bed, and Alice allowed her eyes to feast on the sleeping form of the man who lay amid the tangle of the sheets.

He looked like a lion, she thought—all dark, tawny limbs and golden-dark skin. His ebony head lay cradled in his arms and his breathing was deep and regular. As she sat and watched him she thought how funny it was that you could so easily slip into the pattern of being with a man 24/7. The temporary living-together of being on holiday. Sharing toothpaste and lots of sex.

Yet she had only ever been this close with one man—then and now. The same man—only this time it was different. This time she had lost the inhibition and innocence of youth. She was old enough to recognise that this kind of pleasure was rare indeed and yet through all the moments of joy lingered niggling doubts.

Alice was aware of keeping her feelings dampened down most of the time, of holding her words in check. Wanting to tell Kyros how much she adored him—but somehow she pulled herself back from the brink of doing so just in time. Because Kyros didn't want love—he never had. He liked sex—and she must never lose sight of that, no matter how much Paris tried to seduce her into thinking otherwise.

It was hard to believe that they'd been in the city for five whole days, behaving as lovers had done since the city first became synonymous with romance. They ate oysters in candle-lit restaurants, drank *pastis* on the glittering banks of the Seine, and they walked and walked, through medieval streets, past dusty book-shops and beautiful, darkened churches. At times it felt like a dream—at others, as if she were starring in a soppy movie of her own life. Or maybe a rerun.

Alice kept telling herself that this wasn't reality—just as she kept trying not to think about how quickly the seconds were spiralling away from them. Because the logical progression from thinking about this brief and glorious holiday took her thoughts to a distinctly more uneasy arena—reminding her that time was running out and soon their paths would part once more. And then how would she cope? Having tasted all this pleasure and companionship with a man she had never really stopped loving, could she possibly re-linquish it without regret?

Her thoughts clearing, Alice drifted her eyes over

his face—much softer in sleep—her gaze stopping to rest on the perfect curved shape of his lips, when to her shock they began to move.

'So tell me, what would you like to do this afternoon, *thespinis mou?*'

Alice started. 'I thought you were asleep.'

'I know you did. You were sitting there watching me, and I liked you watching me. Just as I like watching you.' Dark lashes fluttered open to reveal the ebony gleam of his eyes. She was sitting on a wooden table in front of the shutters, a short silk robe tied loosely around her waist, her blonde hair like gold paint spilling over her shoulders and her long legs swinging over the table's edge. She was half colt, half mermaid, he thought lazily. 'If I had a pencil, I would sketch you,' he said.

'Except that we both know you have the drawing ability of a centipede,' she observed tartly.

'Ah, but I might have improved my skills since the last time you saw me attempt to draw something!'

Alice tipped her head to one side. 'And have you?'

Kyros laughed. '*Ohi.* No.' Closing his eyes, he yawned, partly because he was just waking up from some of the best sex he'd ever had, and partly because he didn't want to look into those distracting emerald eyes—because sometimes they made him look at places deep inside himself which he had no desire to see. But it was more than that.

It was disconcerting, this natural cross-referencing

with the past that they did. In a way, Alice knew him better than any woman, and yet the things that she knew were not real or important. Remembering the way he took his coffee or the fact that he had limited artistic abilities had no real bearing on how people lived their lives, did it? They were still poles apart—their experiences completely different—they just happened to have temporarily merged the two in this old-fashioned hotel room in the French capital.

And in two days time you walk away from her— only this time for good.

'What do you want to do this afternoon?' he repeated, wriggling his shoulders restlessly as if shrugging off the unexpectedly dark weight of his thoughts. 'Some sightseeing?'

'You mean this evening? It's almost six o'clock. There's not a lot of afternoon left for sightseeing, Kyros.'

'And whose fault is that?' he questioned softly, glancing at his watch, with a frown.

'Fault?' she teased.

'You know what I mean. Come over here and kiss me, *agape mou.*'

'But that's what I did a couple of hours ago, which put paid to our trip to the *Musée National*—'

'I am bored with museums,' he growled.

'Kyros—we've hardly seen any!'

Black eyes glittered. 'Come here and kiss me,' he repeated stubbornly.

Savouring the moment, Alice walked across the room towards him and went into his arms. The hotel was perfect, though it was not particularly large and certainly not modern. But it was scrupulously clean—and as French as *soupe aux oignons*—with a high, wooden bed and crisp white sheets and a church bell close by which chimed loudly on the quarter. It was situated in the Latin quarter, not far from the pretty *Jardins des Plantes* with its shady avenues of trees, and lawns which you could sprawl on. A welcome oasis in the busy bustle of the French capital. A little like this unexpected interlude with Kyros.

Alice was dreading the moment that it would end—and with it her bubble of happiness. But she had told herself she wasn't going to think that way. She had walked into this with her eyes open—without expectation—and she must not spoil what little time they had left.

She brushed her lips against his. 'How's that?'

'Mmm. Do that again.'

Their mouths were fused in a long and luxurious kiss when Kyros's phone rang and he drew away from her, making a terse imprecation as he reached across the bed to answer it and then began speaking in French.

Alice had studied the language at school, but Kyros was a natural linguist and spoke it so quickly and with such fluidity that she could barely make out a thing he was saying, apart from the occasional word.

'Who was that?' she questioned, when he'd broken the connection.

His dark brows knitted together. 'A man who buys my olive oil. I'm supposed to be having dinner with him tonight.'

'Oh.' Alice tried not to feel hurt. 'Why didn't you mention it before?'

Why indeed? Astonishingly, it had slipped his mind completely. Had he imagined that by the end of the holiday he would have grown bored with her and been eager for a little escape and some male company? How wrong he had been.

He looked at her lying back on the heap of pillows—the dark silk of her robe giving a tantalising glimpse of pale breast beneath. He thought of his dinner engagement with Leon Dupré. The billionaire Frenchman would not be pleased to have a longstanding appointment broken—though Kyros was tempted to do just that, and ultimately it would not matter.

His black eyes narrowed thoughtfully as he thought of Leon's reaction to the woman in his arms. Maybe he'd just had a better idea. A rather more *insightful* idea. How would Alice respond to a man who was obviously loaded and who would inevitably find her attractive? Kyros had deliberately brought her to an understated hotel—he had yet to discover if she was dazzled by wealth. Wouldn't this be an ideal opportunity to find out? 'Do you want to come along with me?' he questioned idly.

Alice forced a smile, still realising how peripheral to his life she really was—but she would achieve precisely nothing by sulking about it. 'Won't he mind me tagging along?'

Mind? As if any man on the planet wouldn't rejoice just to look at her amazing body and emerald eyes. Kyros gave a short laugh. 'Oh, I think Leon will just about cope with it,' he murmured sardonically. He slipped his hand inside her robe and smiled as her eyes darkened. 'Just wear your prettiest dress,' he added huskily as he bent his lips to her neck. 'We'll probably go to a smart restaurant.'

Calling the restaurant 'smart' was probably the understatement of the year, Alice decided as the taxi drew up outside its discreet exterior in the upmarket 8th *arrondissement* and a doorman leapt to attention. Her job sometimes involved travel and she had been to Paris on business—but just one look told her that this place was beyond the means of mere mortals.

'What is the matter, *glyka mou?*' questioned Kyros softly. 'Why do you frown?'

'Are you sure we've got the right address?'

'Of course I am sure—why?'

She turned to him. 'Have you heard of this place?' she asked, and then shook her head as if answering her own question. 'Maybe you haven't. It's, like, *the* most expensive eatery in Paris—the one all the guidebooks bang on about! Why, even a bread roll is likely to cost as much as most people's entire eating budget!' She thought of the likely size of Kyros's olive grove and wondered how much oil it could possibly produce and she bit her lip. 'I do hope your French friend is paying.'

Kyros gave an odd kind of smile. 'Of course Leon will pay—for he is an exceedingly wealthy man. And you must not worry your pretty head about it for a second longer, Alice *mou*.'

The Alice who would once have bristled at being referred to in such a sexist manner seemed a long way away at that moment—another blissful interlude of Kyros's unique brand of love-making seemed to have turned her to one of those stupidly compliant and mushy women who just wanted to gaze adoringly at her lover.

But she still felt distinctly nervous as they followed a stunning woman through an entrance beside which stood a burly security guard whose loose dark clothes did nothing to disguise the fact that he must have done years of body-building.

'And you do think this outfit will be suitable?' she questioned anxiously as they walked into the chandelier-lit room, her hands fluttering over the flouncy skirt of her short silvery-grey dress.

'I told you already a hundred times. The dress is perfect. You are perfect. In fact the only imperfection is that you are wearing a dress at all!' His voice lowered. 'Every man in the room will look at you and wish that they had been doing to you what I was doing just over an hour ago.'

'Kyros!' How was it possible to blush like a naïve schoolgirl at a silky sexual allusion like that—given all the history between them? Because at times that was what she *felt* like…like a woman who… A woman in… Alice swallowed. She wasn't going there. She was *not going there.* She wasn't in love with him—and even if she was, it certainly wasn't reciprocated. *He's going back to Kalfera in a few days,* she reminded herself. *So make the most of your time with him.*

Alice *was* aware of being stared at as they made their way through the tables, following the *maître d'* to a discreet but perfectly placed table at one side of the room. At first she thought that it was Kyros drawing all the attention—the way he did wherever they went—but tonight the eyes seemed to be following *her.*

'*Why* are they looking?' asked Alice with genuine confusion as they took their seats.

Kyros glittered her an odd kind of smile. 'Because you have something that all the accumulated wealth in this room could not possibly buy, *agape mou.* You are young and slim and your hair is naturally blonde and cascades almost to your waist—and there is about you tonight a kind of *glow* which no make-up in the world could create. And although the dress you wear is inexpensive, you wear it well—better than the countless couture creations in this room.' He lowered his voice. 'And because I am not alone in wanting to remove it.'

'What is this you are saying to make her blush so, you *boulevardier?*' came a voice of mocking laughter.

'Leon, your timing is as perfect as always,' said Kyros drily, and Alice looked up to see an impossibly handsome man wearing a superbly cut suit.

'Ah, but that is the secret of my success, *mon ami*— and very possibly yours!'

With his dark eyes and flirtatious smile and a faintly cynical and mocking air, Leon was very obviously French—and as Kyros stood up to greet him he said something in his native tongue which caused the Greek to utter something terse in reply.

This should be interesting, thought Alice—as she smiled and put her hand out to be shaken, but instead the Frenchman lifted it to his lips, blithely ignoring Kyros's glower of rage.

'So where has he been hiding *you?*' teased Leon.

'You make me sound like a caterpillar underneath a leaf!' protested Alice, and he laughed.

'Ah, the charm of the Englishwoman,' Leon purred. 'There is nothing like it!'

'Let's order, shall we?' questioned Kyros, looking even more irritated.

'So you buy olive oil from Kyros, do you, Leon?' questioned Alice chattily, once the waiter had taken their order and the sommelier had poured them an inch of pale golden wine into glasses tall as poppies.

'I do,' agreed Leon. 'And it is the very best olive oil in the world.'

'Leon owns a number of restaurants around France,' said Kyros. 'In fact, he owns this one.'

Alice looked around, her eyes widening. 'Are you serious?'

Leon smiled. 'But of course. *C'est vrai!* And do you know that restaurants no longer fight for the best wine vintages, but for the best oils—for that is how discerning customers now judge them?'

Alice shook her head. 'I didn't know that, no. You must be doing well,' she said, with a sunny smile at Kyros. 'And your olive oil must be superb if you're selling it to an establishment like this—I can't wait to taste it!'

Leon frowned as a look passed between the two men.

'You haven't told her?' the Frenchman asked.

'Told me what?' demanded Alice.

Kyros placed his hand over hers, olive fingers sensuously moving over her skin, making her wish for nothing more than that they could be alone again. 'Oh, just how well my business is doing these days,' he murmured. 'You know that I do not like to boast.'

Alice opened her mouth to say that there were certain areas when he certainly *did* like to boast—

particularly in the bedroom—but she guessed that now was neither the time or the place.

'What else haven't you told her?' Leon was asking softly.

'How good the lobster is,' answered Kyros, his soft tone underpinned with grit as another look passed between the two men.

Alice began to enjoy the evening, helped by the excellent wine and the best food she'd ever eaten—but there was no denying that Leon was a terrible flirt, though she politely kept his attentions at bay. At one point, a woman at the other side of the dining room sent a note over to him, via one of the waiters.

'Tell her no,' he said, after flicking his dark eyes over it briefly.

'Would it be rude to ask what was in it?' asked Alice curiously once the waiter had gone.

'Let me guess—an invitation to her bed?' queried Kyros.

'*Bien sûr!* But the only woman whose bed I am interested in sharing will be sharing it with someone else tonight.' Leon shrugged, his dark eyes gleaming as they roved carelessly over Alice's blonde hair. 'So why don't you swap your men, *ma belle* Alice? Paris is a lot closer than Kalfera.'

At this point Kyros's patience snapped. He looked at Alice and her pink and gold beauty, at the hair which tumbled down around her slender shoulders.

He thought of what Leon—one of France's most

eligible bachelors—would like to do to her. What he still might do, once Kyros had returned to Kalfera. Because the Frenchman was right—Paris *was* much closer. And if not Leon, it would be someone else—someone who would gaze at her beautiful body, someone who would take off her clothes and...

Ohi! He could not and would not bear it!

At this, he rose to his feet, his shadow falling over the table like some symbolic force of darkness. 'I think you overstep the mark, my friend,' he said with soft menace.

Leon looked confused. 'But usually—'

'Usually be damned! This time it is different—do you understand that, Leon? For this is the woman I am intending to make my wife.'

After an initial look of shock, the Frenchman began to murmur abject apologies mixed up with flowery congratulations, but Alice hardly heard a word he was saying—she was too busy staring at Kyros in utter disbelief, scarcely able to comprehend that he had come out with such a dramatic and unexpected statement.

'Shall we go, *thespinis mou?*' he questioned silkily.

In a dazed state Alice nodded and scrambled to her feet. Now was not the time to ask Kyros just what he thought he was playing at—and quite frankly his face was so thunderously angry that she didn't dare risk him losing his temper in the middle of the city's most lavish restaurant. 'It was lovely to have met you, Leon.'

'*Enchanté, mademoiselle,*' said Leon softly, but she noticed that this time he didn't attempt to kiss her hand.

But when they reached the car it was a different matter. 'Are you going to tell me what that was all about?' she demanded as their driver held the door open and she slid onto the back seat.

Did she think he intended to discuss his private life with a stranger listening in? 'When we get back to the hotel,' he said shortly.

'Kyros—'

'Not now,' he growled.

She supposed that he had a point—and it would be embarrassing if he turned round and told her that it had been a device to get Leon off her back. Not just embarrassing, either. For hadn't her heart leapt with a wild and dizzy kind of joy when he had come out with the words she seemed to have been waiting for all her adult life—but never in a million years had expected him to say?

'Just answer me one thing,' she said stubbornly. 'Did you mean what you said?'

'Yes.'

Alice's mind was teeming with questions as the car drove them back to their hotel. She followed Kyros into their room and it wasn't until the door had closed behind them that she gave in to her feelings.

Heatedly, Alice flung her handbag onto the bed, not

caring that the lipstick and hairbrush went flying with a clatter onto the floor. 'What the hell is going on?'

'I asked you to marry me.'

'Why?'

Why indeed? Because in the heat of a dark and overpowering sexual jealousy he had been unable to tolerate the thought of anyone else possessing Alice as he had done. Yet even Kyros recognised that it would be foolhardy to tell her *that*.

'Why not a Greek woman?' she questioned. 'You told me that was what you would do—that your future was all mapped out with a woman who would give you lots of sons.'

He turned away from her critical gaze to study the night-time roofs of the city—the sprinkle of stars and the distant sounds of Parisian revelry. And when he turned back his face was sombre, like a mask worn in a Greek play.

'I have tried relationships with women of my own nationality,' he said carefully, 'both from the mainland and from the island itself, but...' He shrugged his broad shoulders. What had seemed such a good idea in theory had proved anything but. How could he begin to explain that what he thought he had wanted had not been what he had wanted at all? And why should he have to—for wasn't Alice's single state an indication that her own relationships had not worked out either?

'Maybe my time in England changed me more than

I realised at the time. Maybe it made my expectations of a relationship different.'

'So why me?' she repeated—because this was as close as Kyros had ever come to revealing his feelings.

Kyros felt the heavy pounding of his heart—but the weight of his words was beginning to press down on him. 'Because we are good together,' he said starkly. 'You know we are.'

Alice waited. 'And that's it?'

'Isn't that enough?' His black eyes were unsmiling. Did she want for him to continue to paint the truth for her in all its bleak and unsatisfying hues? Couldn't she accept that the nature of life meant compromise? 'Look at your life, Alice—and then compare it to what I am offering you.'

She drew back a little—as if droplets of cold water had hit her unexpectedly in the face. 'What's *wrong* with my life, Kyros?'

'There is nothing *wrong* with it, *agape,*' he said steadily. 'Some would say that you have made a great success of it.'

'Why, thanks very much,' she said sarcastically.

'You have a good job, and an apartment in London—a thing which a lot of people aspire to.' His dark eyes pierced her. 'But where do you see it all going?'

It was something she tried not to do—to glance into an unknown future and its potentially scary landscape. 'I try to live in the present,' she said. 'I told you that.'

'Where?' Kyros demanded, as if she had not spoken, for the Greek way of looking at the world was different—it always had been. They did not deny the ongoing tragedy and disruption of life or its fundamental conflicts. 'Where do you see yourself in five years, Alice? Or in ten? Maybe you will have been promoted and been given a pay-rise—but you will never be a rich woman, for you do not work for yourself.'

'And maybe I don't want to be a rich woman!' she defended.

'No? Then you will have to live with the consequences of that, particularly if you choose to stay in London. You will trade up to a two-bedroom apartment, but it is unlikely that you will make the jump to a bigger one. You will be at the mercy of your mortgage for the rest of your life, until you are an old woman.'

His hard black eyes challenged her to deny the truth of his words and Alice took in a sudden jerk of air, indignant at his damning assessment. 'Aren't you discounting another scenario?'

'Am I?'

'I might meet someone.' Alice swallowed. It was tough for a woman to come out with stuff like this. It made you sound like you were pinning your dreams on it. As if you'd thought it through—like a teenager who had drawn pictures of her wedding dress in the margins of her school book. 'I might meet someone and get married and move out to the country—'

'But you won't meet someone. You know you won't,' said Kyros softly. 'Not someone like me.'

It was an intensely arrogant thing to say and yet wasn't Kyros merely voicing a thought she'd had herself a million times before? Alice opened her mouth to say that maybe she didn't want to meet someone like him—except that surely her very presence in this room would make a mockery of such a statement.

'No one will thrill you the way that I do, Alice,' he continued mercilessly. 'No one will match you on the many levels that I do. We know that we are intellectual equals and we have known each other a long time. You have seen a glimpse of how it could be and you will never find that with another man. And deep down you know that—just as you know something else.' His black eyes were suddenly hard. 'Turn down this opportunity and you will spend the rest of your life regretting it. Growing old while you think of what might have been.'

Alice flinched, but the image he painted sprang all too clearly to the forefront of her mind. A white-haired woman with an empty, aching heart. 'That's a harsh, terrible thing to say!' As if he were putting a curse on her!

'Is it? But sometimes the truth *is* harsh,' he ground out, aware that he was withholding some of it from her.

But he was ruthless enough to see that such an action was necessary. He wanted her, and he knew that she wanted him too—so why would he do or say anything which might jeopardise that? The rough edges could always be smoothed over later.

Alice shook her head. 'And what am I supposed to do on this remote island of yours?'

He withheld a smile of triumph, even though her question told him that he was poised for victory. 'I told you once before,' he said softly. 'It is not some unin-habited backwater with no means of communication. There is nothing to stop you forging a role for yourself there—to find some kind of work, if that is what you should desire.'

'I don't speak Greek, Kyros.'

'You will learn,' he soothed. 'It is true that it is not the easiest of languages—'

'You don't say!'

'But you are an intelligent woman, Alice, and you have the ability to master it.'

Alice shook her head, trying to tell herself that it was a crazy suggestion, that she'd be out of her mind to go through with it. Because there had been one notable omission during all his inducements to marry him. Not a single word of love had passed his lips—not one intimation that she had captured his heart.

'You're asking me to give up too much, Kyros.' But a voice inside her head reminded her that Kyros had never been a man to express emotion. Alice bit her lip.

Maybe it was better to settle for what was real, rather than what was unreachable. 'Much too much,' she said, as if trying to convince herself.

'Am I?' Ruthlessly, he pulled her into his arms and stroked his fingers along the alabaster-pale skin of her cheek. 'Think about it, *agape mou*—do you really want to let all this go?'

His proximity weakened her. His touch undermined all her good intentions—or maybe she was just allowing it to. Maybe that was the coward's way out—of wanting him to kiss her into submission, so that she could let her feelings take over and swamp down the voice of common sense and reason?

Briefly, Alice closed her eyes and when she opened them again it was as if her vision had cleared. *Think of the alternative,* she urged herself. Of turning him down and Kyros going, only this time…this time she would never see him again—she knew that with a kind of bone-shaking certainty.

But this time it would be worse because she would not have all the bright promise of an unknown future to console her. Like some dark Greek tragedy, she could see what a future without Kyros would be like—and it would be bleak in every sense of the word. Because she was older now, and wiser. She was no longer labouring under the illusion that there were hundreds of men like her Greek lover lurking round every corner. Not even one…

His fingertips were now drifting down her upper

arms—not an area she had previously thought of as an erogenous zone, but Kyros seemed to have the ability to make everything he touched seem erogenous. An ebony spark glinted in the depths of his eyes and his mouth was faintly mocking—as if he wanted all this to be over so that he could get down to the serious business of kissing her.

Could she bear to say goodbye to him a second time? That was the bottom line.

Alice's teeth sank into her bottom lip and Kyros knew what her answer would be, even before she had formed it.

'Yes, Kyros,' she said. 'I will marry you.'

CHAPTER SIX

'ALICE, darling, are you *sure* you're doing the right thing?'

'Mum, I'm positive!' Alice stared into the mirror one last time as if checking to make sure that her eyes weren't deceiving her.

Could that cool, dreamy bride who stared back really be her? The woman in floaty cream organza, a fragrant camellia weaved into her hair and a tight bundle of those same flowers waiting downstairs—starry against their dark, glossy leaves and tied with a length of silk-satin ribbon.

Was it the power of her wedding finery which had transformed her into someone who looked like a stranger to her, or was it the hope which still flared in her heart—that she and Kyros could live happily ever after? She turned away from the mirror. 'Anyway, you *like* Kyros—you know you do.'

Her mother frowned. 'Yes, I *do* like Kyros,' she said

dutifully. 'But your father and I were aware how hurt you were when he went away the first time.'

'Oh, we were both too young,' Alice put in quickly, marvelling at the powers of self-deception and her own ability to rewrite history—to try to convince the world that she wasn't making the biggest mistake of her life. As though Kyros walking away the first time had all been part of some grand master-plan! 'Anyway, that was then—this is now.'

'I understand that, dear,' said her mother. 'But this has all happened so quickly—and your father and I are naturally concerned for your happiness.'

'But I *am* happy, Mum. I promise you that. I want nothing more than to be Kyros's wife,' said Alice huskily, the words spoken straight from the heart, and she saw her mother look momentarily mollified as she gave her hat one final adjustment.

The time between accepting Kyros's unexpected proposal of marriage that night in Paris—to the morning of their wedding had passed by in a blur of organisation and arrangements. Part of her had wanted to just slip away and get married in secret—but she knew her parents would be heartbroken if she did something like that. And wouldn't that be sending out the message that what they were doing was in some way shameful?

The first thing Alice had done had been to hand her notice in at work, which had been much harder than she'd anticipated—particularly as they had tried to persuade her to stay. The carrot of a directorship in a couple of years' time had been dangled in front of her, but Alice hadn't allowed herself to be tempted, her career suddenly paling against the dazzle of what Kyros represented and was offering her.

She'd arranged for a letting agency to find someone to rent her flat. That had been her safety net, a precaution taken in case it *didn't* work out—that she had somewhere to come back to. Fleetingly, she found herself wondering whether most brides went into their marriages with such cynical eyes.

While she had shopped for clothes and chosen the menu and all the other seemingly endless details, which even the smallest wedding demanded, Kyros had made arrangements with the Greek Embassy, so that the marriage would be properly legal in both countries. Afterwards, he had flown to Kalfera—to 'make ready' his home for her.

And if Alice had needed any confirmation that she was doing the right thing, his absence drove the point right home. She missed him terribly. Already. The warmth of his hard body in her bed at night. The shivering sensation of knowing he was there. The pleasure she took just from talking to him.

Imagine if he *wasn't* coming back? she found herself thinking—and the thought of it terrified her. How could it be that his impact on her life should be so profound after such a short space of time? And did that mean it would keep on growing and growing, so that one day she would be unable to survive without him—like a piece of mistletoe that had fallen from the oak tree which sustained it?

Well, she must make sure it *didn't* happen—that would be her wedding-day intention. To remain true to herself, no matter what.

Alice reached the bottom of the stairs to see her father looking at her, his expression of concern giving way to one of undeniable paternal pride.

'You look…beautiful, Alice.'

Alice felt as if she wanted to cry. 'Thank you, Dad.'

He nodded. 'Let's go,' he said gruffly.

They had decided on a civil ceremony in a nearby hotel with an early lunch arranged afterwards, before flying out to Kalfera for their honeymoon.

There were few guests—a decision which had arisen both out of choice and of necessity. Just Alice's parents, along with Kirsty and another friend, who were to be their witnesses. It had been too last-minute for Kyros's father to attend—although Kyros hadn't seemed that keen for him to make the journey. Kyros's brother and his wife had twin babies to cope with, and they'd only recently flown back to their home in New York after their own wedding.

Alice found herself strangely disappointed that none of the Pavlidis family would be present—as if their non-attendance made it somehow less significant. 'You do realise that I've never met Xandros—let alone his wife?' she'd said to Kyros.

'But you will,' he had replied. 'You will.'

Alice wondered when. She knew that Xandros hadn't been to Kalfera for years—and somehow couldn't imagine herself and Kyros paying his brother a visit to their home in New York. Why not? As if once she set foot on the fabled island of Kalfera it would swallow her up and she'd never be seen again? But that was crazy, wasn't it? She was marrying Kyros and he…he…

He *what?*

What *did* her husband-to-be think of her—*really* think of her? she thought with sudden alarm as the car pulled up in front of the hotel. And why had she not had the courage to come right out and ask him? Because if he told her he didn't think he could ever properly love her, then pride would not allow her to go through with it. *And I can't bear not to go through with it! I have enough love for both of us.*

Alice swallowed against the sudden debilitating dryness in her throat, putting her anxiety down to nerves. Of course she was nervous—brides were allowed to be nervous! It was just that in her case she wasn't allowed to admit it—not to anyone—as if an admission of that kind would open up the floodgates to people telling her that she must be out of her mind.

To her relief, she saw Kirsty waiting on the steps of the hotel, decked out in a summer dresses with a feathery little creation on top of her head and a great big smile all over her face. At least she hadn't ques-

tioned her logic, but it was different with friends—
Kirsty herself had been a victim of Kyros's powerful
charm. She would only have questioned Alice's sanity
if she'd turned him down!

'He's not here yet.' Kirsty's words greeted her, and
then she sighed. 'Oh, Alice—you look absolutely
stunning! A true contender for bride of the year!'

Not if I get stood up, thought Alice wryly, but at that
moment an enormous low black car pulled up and she
hated herself for the overwhelming sense of relief she
felt.

Kyros was here!

Behind the faintly tinted glass, she could see the
familiar hard, dark profile. His black hair looked
ruffled—as if he had raked his hand back through it
in that impatient way he had—and his body language
was tense. Was Kyros as nervous as she was?

'Why, you're already wearing a wedding ring!' ex-
claimed Kirsty as she lifted up Alice's left hand to
examine the gleaming, pale gold band on her finger.

'It's tradition,' said Alice hurriedly. 'When a couple
become engaged, the man and the woman both wear
their wedding rings on their left hand—and then
switch them to the right hand after the marriage.'

'And no engagement ring, either!' observed Kirsty
disappointedly, her voice carrying down the steps.

'That's because we do things differently in Greece,'
came Kyros's silky voice from behind them. 'Our
customs are not the same as yours.'

Did Alice imagine the sudden chill in the air as they turned round—or was it her own sense of realisation of the magnitude of what she was about to enter into? That they might be marrying in this rather smart hotel—but she would be leaving it far behind to enter into a culture that somehow had never seemed quite so foreign as it did at that moment.

'Hello, Alice, *thespinis mou,*' said Kyros softly, his black gaze meeting hers with a soft blaze of approval which suddenly made all her doubts dissolve.

He turned to her parents then, his manner oddly formal. 'You know that it is also a tradition in my country to ask the father of the bride for her hand on the morning of the marriage?' he said quietly.

There was a brief pause before Alice's father smiled. 'And you have it, Kyros—along with my blessing. All I ask is that you look after her.'

A long look passed between the two men. 'You have my word, sir.'

The wedding passed in a blur of symbolism and ceremony—given an extra twist by the Grecian element—and none of it felt quite real. Afterwards there were glasses of champagne, which Alice did not want to drink, and fancy food she had no appetite for.

'My wife,' said Kyros silkily, catching her fingers and lifting them to his lips. 'You look enchanting.'

'Thank you.'

He liked the way she had lowered her eyelids, as if she were role-playing the part of demure spouse. Was that to conceal the sexual hunger and the passion from her eyes? His voice dipped. 'And I cannot wait to be alone with you.'

'Me, neither,' said Alice unsteadily, hoping that her words sounded convincing. Because she couldn't quite shake the feeling that this was her last taste of normality—as if she were about to board a big ship and sail far, far away. Despite the air-conditioning in the hotel, her brow felt clammy with a cold kind of sweat—and unobtrusively she dabbed at it with her napkin. *It's only Greece, for heaven's sake,* she told herself sternly—*not Mars!*

Before they were due to leave, she went to an upstairs room to change—managing to slip away before her mother or her friends could accompany her. Because maintaining the façade of normality was proving to be hard work and she just wanted to get away from all the curious eyes. She felt as if she were walking a tightrope between what was expected of her, and the way she really felt.

And when she reappeared—with the camellia taken from her hair and the organza dress replaced with a simple silk dress in scarlet, not a colour she usually wore—she saw Kyros's eyes narrow.

She wondered if he was aware that red was the colour of love and fidelity—that some Greek brides even wore red veils. And she wondered whether he would pick up on the silent message she was sending him—but he said nothing.

A nerve was beating at Kyros's temple as they drove off towards the airport. The day had proved more difficult than he had anticipated and the phone call from Kalfera had not helped.

He turned to look at Alice. Even in the dim light of the limousine, her face looked pale against the scarlet of her going-away dress, her green eyes startlingly huge. She was utterly beautiful, he thought.

He brushed a finger over her lips. 'Happy?' he questioned softly.

It was the traditional query from groom to bride—but it seemed ill considered under the circumstances and Alice felt slightly wrong-footed. Was his memory so short, she wondered—or merely selective? Hadn't she asked him the same question of his newly married twin brother and hadn't his unsettling reply stuck in her mind?

'Everyone can be happy for a while,' he had said. 'Whether it will last, who knows?'

'Of course I am,' she said, and forced a smile—though her face felt stretched like a piece of elastic after so many hours of maintaining that smile. 'Just a bit tired, that's all. How long is it going to take us to reach Kalfera?' She stared out of the window. 'And you do realise that this is the wrong direction for Heathrow?'

'But we aren't going to Heathrow, *agape mou*—since scheduled flights would involve a change, and a wait at Athens. There would be many hours of hot and sticky travel—not advisable for a bride who is already weary.' He met the question in her eyes with a hard smile as he prepared himself for the ones which would follow his next statement. 'So we're taking a private jet.'

'Ha ha.' She looked at him. 'Very funny. Where *are* we going—really?'

A smile briefly curved the corners of his mouth. In her a way her naïveté was touching. At least no one would be able to accuse Alice of marrying him for his money. 'I am serious, *glyka mou.*'

'But private jets are—'

'A necessity when you live on an island,' he interjected softly.

'You mean it's *your* plane?'

'Of course.'

'But you make *olive oil,* Kyros—not gold!'

It occurred to him that sometimes the shared past could be more of a hindrance than a unifying factor. She was his wife, yes—but she must learn to have respect for his judgement. And did she not realise from the tone of his voice that he no longer wished to discuss it?

'My business is doing extremely well,' he said smoothly. 'I told you that in Paris. To the gourmet diner—olive oil *is* like liquid gold.' His eyes were mocking now. 'And I am a man of simple tastes, *agape mou*—I spend my wealth on what makes life comfortable. Believe me when I tell you that you will grow to love having my plane at your disposal.'

Alice sat back in her seat, confused now and very slightly bewildered. A private jet was a lot to land on someone—even if it *was* your only extravagance, as Kyros had hinted. But it was more than that. It was Kyros's sense of ownership.

My plane, he had said—when weren't married people supposed to share everything? Or was that just a slip of the tongue—an old way of speaking which he hadn't got round to changing? Like saying *we* from now on, instead of *I*. Perhaps everything had happened so quickly that neither of them had become used to the brand-new language of coupledom.

'I've never been on a private jet before,' she said.

'Well, that's good.' For the first time that day, he felt the heady rush of anticipation. 'I think you will approve—because none of the normal strictures apply, Alice *mou*. I can dismiss the crew for us to have the cabin to ourselves.' He trickled a finger thoughtfully over the scarlet silk which was moulded against her thigh. 'Would you like to consummate our marriage high in the clouds, *thespinis mou?*'

Was it Alice's jangled nerves which made her blanch at his suggestion? Or was it the way he said it, following straight on from his extraordinary revelation about the plane? As if she were some sort of trophy to hang up inside it? Surely that was a disrespectful way to treat his new wife—to make love to her with the crew knowing *exactly* why they had been banished from the cabin?

'You mean making me a member of the Mile High club?' she questioned tartly. 'Since I assume you're already among that group.'

Kyros laughed. 'What a prude you sound, Alice!'

Alice's lips trembled. 'So you *are* a member?'

His black eyes glittered. 'Do not ask me questions if you cannot bear to hear the answers,' he warned softly. 'I do not ask you about the lovers you have had in your bed in the ten years since I've been away.'

'Maybe I haven't had any!'

'Ah, Alice.' He lifted her fingers to his lips and sucked on one provocatively and when he released it, his mouth curved into a mocking smile. 'Alice, Alice, Alice! You need not tell me what you think I want to hear! Your body was made for sex, your appetites fine-tuned to enjoy it. And remember you had the best tutor available. I am confident that no man who came after me would have pleasured you quite so thoroughly as I did.' His eyes hardened then, and so did his voice. 'I just do not wish to know about them all.'

Alice opened her mouth to contradict him and tell him that there had in fact only been one other lover since he'd left—and a woefully inadequate one, come to that. But something stopped her and she wasn't sure if it was pride or indignation. He would assume she'd been living like a nun—because of *him*—while he boasted openly of having made love to women on his private jet!

'You really are an arrogant bastard,' she said softly.

'I know. It's what makes me so…' his fingers slipped beneath her dress until he found the cool band of flesh which lay above her silk stocking-top and he felt her shiver as he began to slide her panties down '…irresistible.'

'Kyros—'

'Don't fight it just for the sake of fighting it, *thespinis mou*. I chose this car specifically. The driver can neither see nor hear us and we have time enough before we reach the airfield. We can wait until we are on Kalfera if you insist on propriety—but it will seem like an unbearably long journey.'

Briefly, he allowed his thoughts to stray to what lay ahead of them and he felt a darkness invade his soul. But surely the woman in his arms could take some of that darkness away, with her bright beauty and her passion? Couldn't he lose himself in her in a way which was unique? 'I want you, Alice,' he said unsteadily. 'And I want you now.'

And Alice was taken aback by the sudden power of his kiss.

CHAPTER SEVEN

'WE'RE here,' said Kyros suddenly as the car rounded another bend and Alice gave a little gasp as she caught her first glimpse of his island home.

'Oh, Kyros,' she said, her voice soft as she stared up at it, still with that faintly dream-like sensation clinging to her skin. 'It's so…so…*beautiful.*'

The house stood on a hill—a large, two-storey stone villa, surrounded by lemon-studded trees and overlooking the turquoise waters of the Mirtoan Sea.

Kyros had driven them there in a gleaming silver car, which had snaked its way up the mountainous roads, passing fragrant pine forests and leaving faint clouds of dust in their wake.

The top-of-the-range sports car had been waiting for them on the small runway when they'd landed from England in the blistering heat of the afternoon— the keys handed over by what had looked almost like a small deputation of officials to Alice. A group of black-eyed men who had looked at her curiously as she had smoothed her hair back from her warm face and said hello in faltering Greek.

Alice found herself remembering her new husband telling her that he was a man of simple tastes—somehow managing to cite that as a reason for owning his own private jet! So where did this powerful car fit in with such simplicity? Or a house which must surely command the very best view on the island?

But now was not the time to ask him. First impressions were important and Alice wanted hers to be rosy and to stay in her mind that way for ever. And so she pushed away the niggling thought that all was not as it seemed. She wanted to love the island as much as Kyros did and to understand it, too. This place to which she was a complete stranger and where now she must make her new life.

Kalfera.

How often had she imagined what it must be like?

When they'd been at university she had longed for an invitation to come and stay here—but none had come, despite her not-very-subtle hints. Who could have imagined that ten years on she would find herself here as a new bride, with Kyros at her side? Why, once this would have been her dream scenario—so why had she been plagued with butterfly nerves all through the sometimes turbulent flight to the island?

'See down there,' Kyros said softly as they got out of the car and breathed in the hot and fragrant air. 'That's the bay where Xandros and I used to swim.'

It seemed a long way down to where a curve of sapphire was edged with a blinding ribbon of silver sand. She could see steps carved out of stone leading from the house down to the beach. 'Where you cut your leg on the rock and bled everywhere?'

'Who told you that?'

'You did, of course. Years ago.' Almost imperceptibly, she brushed her fingertips against his thigh. 'And you've got a scar to prove it, remember?'

His hard profile relaxed into a smile. Hadn't she often traced its jagged line with the delicate tip of her tongue, as if doing that would melt away its hard white ridge? 'I'm surprised you can remember a little detail like that, *kardia mou.*'

She could remember every single thing about him—but she wasn't going to tell him that. Such encyclopaedic knowledge ran the risk of making her sound weak and cloying, and Kyros did not want that kind of devotion.

'Who were those men on the airfield?' she questioned as he opened the boot of the car.

'Just Stavros and Christos and a couple of their cousins.' He removed a small bag and turned to meet her eyes. 'Why?'

'Oh, I don't know. They seemed…'

'What did they seem, Alice?' questioned Kyros softly.

'Deferential, I guess.'

'They work for me. It is the way of things.'

'At the olive refinery?'

'No. In one of my offices.'

'Why, how many offices do you have?' she joked.

He knew he was going to have to tell her before someone else did. But not today. 'Don't worry about it,' he said easily. 'You're tired, Alice.'

And something allowed her to relax and to let Kyros be all protective—because he was right about the tiredness. In fact, she was bone-weary—partly due to the tension she'd felt prior to the wedding and partly due to the times he'd made love to her since then.

In the car on the way to the airfield.

On the plane. Not once, but twice—with Kyros kissing her gasps of pleasure quiet during the most erotic encounter of Alice's life. But afterwards she had sensed a change of mood in him. Some deep air of melancholy which had settled on him. She had been stroking his hair with a certain tenderness and he had been letting her and she had been about to ask him what was on his mind, when the pilot had made an announcement over the intercom and in the rush to adjust their clothes the moment had been lost.

Kyros shut the car door and glanced up towards the house.

'Shall I help you carry the suitcases in?' Alice questioned.

'*Ohi*. That will be taken care of.' He smiled. 'Someone else will do it. Your days of carrying suitcases are over, Alice.'

But Alice felt a sudden intimation of foreboding shimmer its way over her skin. He made her sound like someone else. Someone she didn't recognise. A woman who would no longer have to carry her own suitcases...

A sound behind made her turn to see a middle-aged couple emerging from the house and she smiled as they approached. This must be the couple Kyros had told her about—who took care of the house when he was away on business.

'Alice, I want you to meet Sophia and Yiannis, who make this house run smoothly,' said Kyros and added something in rapid Greek before switching back to English. 'Sophia does most of the cooking while her husband oversees the gardeners.'

Oversees the gardeners? And how many gardeners would that be? Rather dazedly, Alice shook hands with them both.

'Kalispera,' she said, with a smile.

'We welcome you, Kyria Pavlidis,' said Sophia, and Alice found herself wondering why the housekeeper's expression was so wary—or was it just that her fatigue was making her imagine things?

She stood there like an obedient spouse during a brief interchange between Kyros and Sophia, but then Kyros put his arm around her shoulder and pulled her against him and she sank into his hard body with a sudden sense of relief.

'Shall we go inside, Alice *mou?*' he questioned softly.

She looked up at him. 'Yes, please.'

He thought that he had never seen her look quite so sweet or so vulnerable as she did at that moment—and he felt a twist of pain, though he kept his face impassive as he caught her hand in his. The sound of the cicadas whirring around and the heavy beat of the sun filled his senses and they had almost reached the door when, without warning, he bent and scooped her up into his arms, and Alice let out a squeal.

'Kyros! What do you think you're doing?'

'You don't know?' Dark brows were arched. 'Why, I am carrying you over the threshold, as tradition demands.'

'But not Greek tradition?'

'Alas, no. For we do not have evil spirits hiding in the ground in Greece as you do in England.' His voice softened. 'I simply would not permit it.'

His words made her feel dizzy as a torrent of conflicting emotions threatened to overwhelm her. The sensation of being in Kyros's arms made her feel both kittenish and sensual as he stroked enticingly at her bottom, but the sense of the unknown was pretty daunting as he carried her into the house.

'It's so cool,' she said, looking around as he set her down onto the marble floor, and she slipped off her sandals to feel the cold stone beneath her bare feet.

'That's because these houses were built with thick

walls to withstand the fierce burn of the summer heat—though in winter it can be cold, which is why we have fires.'

'Fires? In Greece?' Alice shook her head. 'Oh, Kyros—there's so much I don't know. So much I want to learn.'

'And I will teach you.' He dipped his head to brush his lips against hers. 'Where would you like to start?'

A little tremor ran through her body as his desire communicated itself to her. 'What about Sophia and Yiannis?' she whispered.

'Yannis will be tending to the garden and Sophia preparing our first dinner here.' The lips lingered. 'Shall we go upstairs and I will show you our bedroom?'

Alice nodded as she tasted the warmth of his breath against hers, anticipating more of his particular brand of love-making and yet slightly overwhelmed by everything which had happened to her that day. 'That would be lovely,' she agreed unevenly.

Kyros's eyes narrowed and he drew back and touched his finger to the paleness of her cheek. 'Or would you like to go down to the beach for a quick swim instead? To feel the sun and the water on your skin?'

'Oh, Kyros. I'd love that—I feel as if I've been inside for so long. Is there time?'

He laughed indulgently. 'Of course there is time. Dinner can be served whenever you want it to be.

Come and let's get changed—have you brought a swimsuit with you?'

'Are you kidding? I've bought five!'

Their spacious bedroom was like something out of a glossy brochure, simply yet sumptuously appointed—with plain white walls and a huge white-covered bed and just a few old and very beautiful pieces of furniture. There was a carved chest of drawers and a curved daybed—but the best bit of all was the view.

Tall windows looked directly out to sea, and there was a wide balcony outside, with a table and chairs and pots of fragrant flowering plants growing there.

Alice had brought a choice of bikinis made in various degrees of skimpiness, but today she was determined to swim and unsure what would be regarded as suitable until she'd settled in a bit more. So she chose a sleek one-piece in vibrant tangerine, which contrasted sunnily with the pale gold of her hair. Pulling on a matching kaftan and a pair of sparkly flip-flops, she went outside to lean over the balustrade as a faint breeze blew gently at her hair.

'Like it?' Kyros came up behind her and put his arms around her waist, nuzzling his mouth at the base of her neck.

'It's unbelievable. The sea's so blue.'

His eyes narrowed against the light. He could detect her faint scent and feel her lush body in the thin fabric of her swimsuit and automatically his body stirred.

Yet, for once, desire did not do what he often demanded of it—which was to obliterate the unwanted thoughts which buzzed around in his head like mosquitoes trapped in a night-time room.

This felt like a part he was playing—yet it was as if he knew the words to the script without having to learn them first. It was not real—and he knew it could not last—but who could blame him for wanting to finish the first act without interruption? 'Then let's go and swim,' he said abruptly.

Stone steps led from the far end of the lower garden all the way down to the shore and Alice followed Kyros down, and when they reached the bottom the sky was beginning to change colour to a deep rose-pink while the sea was growing inky-dark.

Alice peeled off her kaftan and ran straight in—the sand pushing up between her bare toes as it gave way to the warm lick of the waves.

She swam right out before turning to tread water—looking back to where Kyros was sitting on a rock. The view was perfect from here, she thought dreamily. The water, the sand and the man with the majestic rise of the mountain behind. Her gaze travelled upwards and she thought she saw something bright flash on one of the hilltop paths and narrowed her eyes to look there properly, but as she blinked she could see there was nothing.

I'm here, she thought. *I'm married to Kyros—and it feels perfect. This marriage can be anything you want it to be,* she told herself fiercely as she swam around for a while and then struck off back towards the shore.

Kyros watched her. He had known that she'd want to swim. He found himself remembering a day when they had taken the train to the English coast, as students. He recalled her fearlessness at the icy water—the way she had jumped right in. How easily the past could weave into the present, he thought. How memory could distort reality—but just for a moment he would let it.

'You really *are* a mermaid,' he murmured as she emerged dripping from the sea and he pulled her into his arms.

She turned her face upwards. 'That was the best thing I've done in ages!'

He bent and kissed away a drop of salt-water. 'Oh, really?'

Their eyes held and Alice laughed.

'Well, maybe the *second* best thing…'

It was the first time he had seen her truly relaxed all day. 'Come on. Let's go and see what Sophia has prepared for us. Are you hungry?'

'I'm starving,' said Alice honestly and it felt like the first time that she'd wanted food in ages.

As they walked slowly back up the steep steps she experienced the deepest feeling of contentment. If only she could capture that feeling and bottle it—and release the cork whenever she was feeling insecure.

Because surely this feeling of closeness boded better for the future than any words of love could ever do.

People could say things they didn't mean just because they thought you wanted to hear them—but Kyros hadn't done that. He hadn't told her he loved her, which showed that he was no hypocrite. Yet surely you couldn't fake the compatibility she was experiencing right then—the real bond she felt existed between them? Wasn't that more real and more precious than any unrealistic romantic expectations?

When they arrived back at the house they showered and changed before going downstairs to the dinner Sophia had prepared. The table had been laid outside on the terrace and was lit by guttering candles and the fading glow of the setting sun. Purple flowers stood in a small stone vase and sent out a subtly sweet scent as dishes of different foods were laid before them.

Melt-in-the-mouth lamb studded with garlic and scattered with rosemary was joined by lots of different salads. They drank soft Greek wine and afterwards ate a cake made with honey and quince.

'This is absolutely delicious, Sophia,' said Alice, with a shy smile. 'Thank you.'

'*Parakalo,*' said the Greek woman. 'You are welcome.'

And if Sophia was slightly reserved in her manner towards her, then Alice couldn't really blame her. After all, she was the new wife coming into a house where there had been no wife before. A housekeeper would always be wary of another woman entering what must have been her own territory for so long.

They sat in the starlight drinking their coffee and then Kyros took her upstairs to their bedroom, where the shutters were still open and the moon cast a silver path on the wooden floor, and he undressed her in its muted light.

'You look like a goddess,' he breathed as her bright hair tumbled down around her naked body. 'All curves of light and shade. My beautiful goddess.'

'And you are my Greek god,' said Alice almost shyly as she began to unbutton his shirt.

He carried her over to the bed and pulled her down on top of him, tangling his fingers distractedly into the silken ropes of her hair as her soft thighs straddled him. And Alice sank onto him and moved to the rhythm of the oldest dance of all—while Kyros watched her—until at last his head fell back against the pillow and he groaned and said something harsh in his native tongue.

She must have slept—and slept deeply—because when she awoke the room was in pitch darkness, so that at first she thought it must still be night-time. It was only when her eyes began to adjust that she realised Kyros must have got up to close the shutters during the night.

Alice sat up and looked around, but the room was empty—the vacant, rumpled space on the bed next to her the only sign that her husband had slept there. She yawned, and reached out for her watch only to discover that it was already past ten o'clock. She hadn't slept so late in years! Lazily, she stretched her arms above her head.

'Kyros?'

But there was no sound from the bathroom. Alice rose and went to open the shutters, blinking furiously at the intense brightness of the sunlight which flooded in. She stepped out onto the balcony and looked down, but the beach was deserted—the sea an inviting cobalt glitter.

Well, Kyros had obviously wanted to let her sleep—so she would have a quick shower and then go and find him. Her lips curved. And kiss him.

Twisting her damp hair back in a French plait, she put on a yellow sun-dress and a pair of sandals and then went downstairs.

'Hello!' she called. 'Oh, hello, Sophia,' she said as the housekeeper appeared from the direction of the kitchen. 'What a beautiful morning!'

Sophie nodded. '*Ne, kyria.* You would like breakfast?'

'Yes, please—but first I'd like to see Kyros. Where is he, Sophia?'

There was a slight pause. 'Kyrios Pavlidis has gone out.'

Alice felt slightly foolish—not wanting to lose face in front of the other woman, but what choice did she have? 'Do you know where?'

'*Ne, kyria.* To the bank.'

'To the bank,' repeated Alice slowly, and forced a smile. 'If he'd wanted to borrow some money, he could have asked me!'

But the lack of response reminded Alice that jokes were clearly not the way to go—even if they proved a useful way of hiding her hurt that Kyros had disappeared on the first full morning of their honeymoon without leaving her any kind of note.

'You would like breakfast now, Kyria Pavlidis?'

In truth, Alice felt as if any food would choke her—but pride made her give an even brighter smile. 'I'd love some, please, Sophia. May I have it on the terrace?'

'*Ne.* Of course.'

Sunlight dappled through the thick canopy of leaves which overhung the terrace where a table for one had already been set. Alice forced herself to concentrate on the delicious warm smell of pine and the song of unfamiliar birds—but she felt frighteningly alone as she sat there, in her brand-new yellow sundress, with no husband to see it.

She kept expecting him to appear before Sophia brought out the jug of hot, strong coffee—or the fruits and bread—and the thick, dark honey which Sophia told her was made by Kalfera bees. But Kyros did not appear and Alice ate her meal in self-conscious silence.

But afterwards she felt much better and set out to

explore, slightly nonplussed by the fact that the gardens turned out to be something which resembled a massive estate—something she hadn't been expecting at all. But land in Greece was much cheaper than in England, she reasoned.

There were lots of different areas—some growing vegetables and others flowers, while others were more formal, with marble pillars and beautiful statues. And there were seats positioned at various spots, which she suspected had been placed there to maximise the stunning views and sunlight at different points in the day.

She found the swimming pool—with its infinity edge appearing to connect it to the sea—and took her sandals off and sat with her feet dangling into the deliciously cool water, fully expecting Kyros to appear at any moment, and to put his arms on her shoulders and bend down to kiss the back of her neck in a way which always made her shiver with anticipation.

But as the minutes ticked by there was no sign of him and eventually Alice plucked up the courage to go back to the house and find Sophia.

'Did...did Kyros say what time he'd be home, Sophia?'

Had she just broken some unknown social code? For the housekeeper looked as if Alice had just asked her to find her a toy-boy for the day, and shook her head.

'*Ohi,* Kyria Pavlidis. He did not say.'

The subtext being that the master of the house certainly didn't consult his housekeeper about his time-
table, Alice supposed. Nor his wife, it would seem.
Well, she wasn't going to sit around all day waiting
for him, like a pet! She would go down to the beach
with one of the books she'd brought out with her and
which she had rather stupidly thought she wouldn't get
a look at for weeks.

Taking care to apply plenty of sun-cream and to
take a large, floppy hat, Alice asked Sophia to pack her
some bottles of iced water in a cool bag and then she
set off on the path she'd taken yesterday.

But today it was as if someone had flipped a coin
and everything felt different. Although she swam and
although the sea was wonderful—Alice couldn't
settle. The words of her new book blurred into mean-
ingless lines, for a beach could feel like the loneliest
place in the world and, right now, Alice felt like the
only person inhabiting that world.

If she went back to the house and Kyros was still
not back, what could she do? There were no friends
around the corner—no one she could even ring, or ask
around. She felt as trapped as a butterfly which had
just been captured beneath a glass dome.

She was just staring out at the still blue horizon
when she heard a rustle behind her and couldn't help
the automatic leap of her heart as she turned around—
but her smile changed into a look of surprise as she

saw a child peering at her from behind one of the rocks.

It was a little girl, aged about five—a beautiful child, with large, dark eyes and wavy black hair caught up in a white ribbon. Her eyes crinkled at the corners and some whispering fleet of recognition whispered into Alice's memory, before it vanished again.

'Hello,' said Alice. 'I mean *kalispera.*'

'I speak English,' said the little girl, coming out from behind the rock.

'Do you? That's very clever—I wish I spoke Greek.' Alice glanced up at the stone steps. 'Where's your mummy? She might be worried about you.'

'I don't have a mummy.'

Alice's face softened. 'Don't you, darling? Well, what about your daddy, then?'

'You married my daddy,' said the little girl quite clearly.

There was a moment when Alice did that thing of thinking that the little girl must be play-acting or pretending, as children were wont to do. Like pretending they were princesses or fairies. But that moment dissolved as she heard the sound of a woman's voice shouting: 'Olympia! Olympia!' and saw the way the child frowned in response. Something in that frown... something in her eyes.

'Your daddy?' said Alice, like a robot. 'Who told you that?'

'He rang my auntie on your wedding day.'

Alice felt even more confused now—but then memories of Kyros arriving at the hotel flooded back into her mind. Kyros sitting in the car. She remembered seeing his irritated expression and had wondered if that was due to nerves. As if Kyros had ever been nervous in his life. What the hell was going on?

'Olympia!' The woman's voice called out again—more imperiously this time.

'I must go,' said the little girl, and just before she turned towards the steps said, 'What's your name?'

'It's Alice.'

'I'm Olympia,' said the child, a look of appeal in her dark eyes. 'Will you tell Daddy I want to come round soon?' She hesitated, as if she was trying to remember something. 'For tea.'

CHAPTER EIGHT

'Is KYRIOS Pavlidis back yet, Sophia?' Alice was still out of breath from running back from the beach and her kaftan was clinging to her hot and sticky body. 'Or has there been any word from him at all?'

'*Ne, kyria.* He rang to say that he had been held up. That he come back—'

'*Efkaristo,* Sophia,' came a voice from the direction of the house and Kyros walked out onto the terrace, his dark eyes instantly taking in Alice's pinched expression—even though it was shadowed by the wide brim of the hat she wore. 'That will be all, thank you, Sophia.'

'*Ne,* Kyrios Pavlidis. I will see you tomorrow,' said Sophia quickly, and left.

Had he spoken to the housekeeper in English so that his wife would understand, wondered Alice—so that she wouldn't feel more excluded than she did already? Or was he thinking that by dismissing the other woman, then he'd be able to work his particular magic in getting Alice round to his way of thinking? To manipulate her as only he could with his lips and his caresses? Well, this time he was wrong.

Taking the hot hat from her head, she stared at him, thinking that he looked like a stranger in his beautiful cool, linen suit. No, not quite a stranger—but never so *foreign* to her as he did at that moment. *I don't know you,* she thought suddenly. *I don't know you at all. Maybe I never did.*

'So when were you going to put me in the picture, Kyros?' she asked slowly. 'Or weren't you going to bother?'

There was a pause as Kyros expelled a long breath of air. 'Who told you?'

Alice gave a short laugh of disbelief. He had asked the classic question of the man who had been caught out. It was more usual for the subject matter to be infidelity—but in a way, wasn't this worse? Wasn't a secret child much harder to bear than a mistress? 'What does it *matter* who told me? Surely the only important fact is that you didn't.'

'But it is only money!' he bit out. 'And I only bought the damned thing last month.'

Alice stilled. Was she going insane—or was this just a terminal communication breakdown, when they both seemed to be speaking different languages?

'Bought *what?*' she questioned, in a low voice. 'I'm talking about the daughter you haven't bothered to tell me about—what are *you* talking about?'

The breath caught in his throat and then Kyros winced, his eyes briefly closing, and when he opened them again the expression within their ebony depths was stony. 'I think you will understand the relevance of my query this time. How did you find out about Olympia?'

Hadn't there been some tiny, stupid part of her which had been hoping he'd deny it? That he might indulgently explain that his young neighbour had always hero-worshipped him—an explanation which Alice would normally have had no difficulty in accepting. He was just the kind of man that little girls *would* idolise.

But she had seen Olympia's face; something about her eyes and something about her frown. And she had seen the pain and confusion in the child's dark eyes—and had known that she had not been inventing stories. Just as Kyros was not standing there denying that he had a daughter.

'Olympia told me herself.'

'She came here?' he demanded.

'No. I met her on the beach. I went down there for a swim when I awoke and found you gone, without explanation. Who is she, Kyros? Or more importantly— who is her mother?'

Her skin was paper-pale and the emerald eyes were bright and huge in her face and suddenly he was very afraid that she might faint. 'Sit down, Alice.'

'I don't want to sit down!'

'Do you want me to tell you when we are standing facing one another on the terrace, like two adversaries ready to fight?'

'Why, how had you planned to tell me?' she shot back, afraid that the hot tears which were springing at the backs of her eyes would start streaming down her face. And he would *not* see her cry. He would *not*. 'Did you think I'd be more amenable if you enlightened me when we were in the bedroom—thinking that your fantastic love-making would allow you to get off with pretty much anything? A quick kiss, a slow caress and dear old Alice will take whatever I tell her?'

'Do not insult me in such a way!' he snapped.

'Insult *you?* Oh, no.' Alice shook her head, aware that some of her hair was tumbling out of the French plait—all disordered after her sweltering and desperate run up the cliff steps to get back to the house. Even then, hoping against hope that she might have been mistaken. 'Please don't take the moral high ground with me, Kyros. I really don't think you're in any position to do that!'

'Sit down,' he repeated insistently.

Unable to withstand the fierce pressure in his voice—or the shaky feeling in her knees—Alice sank down onto one of the cushioned wicker seats on the terrace. How ironic that just yesterday she had been dining out here beneath the stars, intoxicated by the fragrance of the flowers and the soft, Grecian night and the gleam of promise in the eyes of her new husband. What a sham it had all been.

'So where do you begin?' she questioned. 'Even a man as famously charismatic as you must acknowledge the difficulties in trying to talk your way out of this one.' She bit her lip. 'Or aren't you going to bother trying?'

'Don't you think that every person in this world can look back on various aspects of their behaviour and question it? Have you never done that yourself, Alice—or are you so very perfect?' he demanded. He stared at her, and when no answer came he shook his head. 'When I left you in England, I truly believed that it was for the best of all possible motives. I had seen my own parents' marriage fail—the only one of all my peers to do so. I had seen my mother break one of the greatest social taboos by walking away.'

Why tell her of the pain he had felt when he had hidden it from everyone, even his twin? Two bewildered boys who had both retreated inside themselves—unable to comprehend how a mother could leave her sons for her lover without even a backward glance.

His black eyes were suddenly cold and empty. 'The marriages which worked were the ones between couples who had grown up here. Those were the ones I envied—that was the kind of family framework I wanted. The mother with a meal on the table for her family—not a succession of nannies who were too busy flirting with the local waiters to pay much attention to two wild little boys. Maybe it was too simplistic an explanation—but I imagined that I would find that by coming back here one day and marrying a woman from the island.'

'After you'd played the field, I suppose?'

He saw the appeal in her eyes—but she could not demand to know the truth and then simultaneously shield herself from it. 'Yes, of course. An English bride was not part of my plan—especially not at such a ridiculously young age. After I left London, I settled in Athens—which is where I built up my property portfolio—'

'And that's where you made your money,' said Alice slowly as it all came together in her head. The private jet. The silver car. The big house—and the cluster of men who had met him at the airport and treated him as if he were some kind of god. What an idiot she had been not to have guessed before—or had she simply been duped because he hadn't wanted her to know?

'*Ne.*' His black eyes were watchful. 'Then, when I considered the time to be right—I returned to live in Kalfera.'

Alice could imagine the excitement among the women on the island when the stunning and eligible Greek billionaire moved back there full time—why, it must have been like something out of a Jane Austen novel. 'What happened?' she questioned dully.

How could he explain to Alice, whom he had hurt badly—not once, but now twice—that reality had fallen short of his own expectations? That the ideal woman of his dreams had not existed? He had wanted everything—someone who had grown up on Kalfera and spoke his language and shared his values, yet combined with the kind of pizzazz and sophistication he had found in the European women he had bedded.

'I was introduced to a woman named Katarina—'

'That's Olympia's mother?'

'Yes.'

Alice swallowed. 'So what's she like?'

He didn't correct the tense. Not yet. And how did you tell your wife that the mother of your child was her very antithesis? What conclusions would she draw from that? 'She was very Greek and very lovely.'

'So you found what you were looking for, did you, Kyros?' Had she successfully prevented the pain from distorting her voice or did her face give her away?

Kyros nodded. 'For a while. But then I realised it wasn't going to work between us—not in the long-term. And once I realised that I told her…'

His voice trailed off. No need to ask whether Katarina had taken it badly, thought Alice. Hadn't *she*? What woman wouldn't be bereft when a man like that walked out of her life? Maybe Kyros had left a stream of broken-hearted women all the way across the world.

'So what happened? How did she get pregnant?'

And then she flinched. 'Silly of me. The usual way, I suppose.'

'Let me tell you what happened,' said Kyros quietly. 'When the relationship finished, Katarina left the island—and when she returned a year later it was with a baby. My baby,' he finished.

Alice stared at him. 'You'd known she was pregnant?'

'Of course I didn't know she was pregnant!' he exploded. 'It was not planned.'

'You're saying it was a mistake?'

'I'm saying that I did not intend for Katarina to get pregnant,' he said deliberately.

'But she did?'

He gave his dark head an impatient shake. 'Apportioning blame is pointless, especially now. If a woman decides to get pregnant—then if it is at all possible, she will.'

'It must have been a big deal on a place like this.' She looked at him then, and now she felt that she *was* looking at a stranger. How many more secrets had he concealed from her? 'So what did you do, Kyros? And where is she now?'

'I did the only thing possible, under the circumstances—I offered to marry her.'

Alice was glad that he *had* insisted she sit down, because she suspected that she really might have slumped at this startling new piece of information. 'You've been married before?' she whispered.

Kyros shook his head impatiently. 'You don't think that would have showed up on the legal papers before our own marriage?'

She wanted to tell him not to use words like *our marriage*—such intimate words for something which was essentially a mockery. Why, she had simply been used for his convenience! 'How would I know?' Her voice trembled. 'Maybe you could have bought your way out of it.'

Black eyes pierced her. 'You think that?'

'Why not? You've already shown me that just about anything is possible.' Alice shrugged—as if that might shift the heavy pain which felt as if it were pressing down on her like a lead weight. 'So what happened? I want to hear the rest.'

He wanted to tell her not to judge him so brutally— and then, yes, to kiss away the hurt and pain, to lose himself in that. But a new and shuttered expression in her green eyes warned him away. And there was still that tense and expectant look on her face which told him that she was still waiting to hear the story.

'I wanted to do my duty—to Katarina, and to Olympia. In a small community such as this—to have a child out of wedlock is frowned upon, and that is why I proposed marriage.'

The breath caught in Alice's throat. Wasn't *duty* a hateful word? And then a voice in her head began to mock her—for wasn't *convenient* an even worse one?

Kyros turned his head to stare at the dappled light

playing on the trunk of a tree as the memories came flooding back, stronger now and gathering momentum as they reached their terrible climax. 'Plans for the wedding went ahead.' He stopped then, because emotion was a funny thing. It could hit you no matter how hard you tried to cushion your reaction—and some things never lost their power to shock. He clenched his fists. 'And Katarina was killed in a car crash two nights before the marriage was due to take place.'

Alice started and she looked at him in horror, shaken out of her own sadness by the thought of a young mother being snatched by death in the very prime of her life.

'Oh, Kyros,' she breathed. 'That's awful.'

He turned his head back to look at her. God forgive him, but her compassion made him want to take her into his arms. He wanted her to soothe him. To stroke his hair as she had done on the plane—when for one extraordinary moment he had felt true peace. But the sympathy in her eyes vanished and was replaced by that new, cold look. 'Yes,' he agreed. 'Awful for her, and terrible for Olympia. And for Katarina's parents, of course.'

'You didn't...you didn't bring the baby to live with you?'

'No.' He shook his head. 'It is not the Greek way— not in such circumstances. I had to travel—and could not provide the continuing care and daily routine which Olympia needed—and it was some small comfort to her parents and her sister that they should have her living with them.'

Were her senses becoming more finely attuned after each shattering discovery? Or was Alice just unable to trust Kyros and his motives any more? 'But something has changed?' she said softly.

Black eyes narrowed. Were her powers of perception so great? he wondered. 'Yes,' he agreed heavily. 'Katarina's sister is soon to be married, and her parents themselves are getting old.'

'And a more settled domestic life would improve your case for a custody plea?' Alice guessed. 'Am I right?'

He knew where she was taking this—and could he honestly blame her in the circumstances? 'Not necessarily full custody, no—I have no desire to uproot Olympia, but I would like to see more of her, *ne.*'

'How very convenient, then,' said Alice slowly. 'To come home with a wife.'

'It isn't like that,' he said harshly.

'Isn't it? Then how else do you account for the extraordinary sequence of events which led me to your marital bed, Kyros? And why the hell didn't you *tell* me any of this before—so that at least I would have had some say in the matter? To feel that I had an element of *choice*—rather than being presented with a *fait accompli.* Why didn't you tell me the truth, right from the start?'

'Because I never intended for it to get this far,' he said softly. 'It was never meant to be more than one night in your bed!'

Alice felt faint. Well, that certainly told her! 'And then?'

She wanted the truth, did she? Well, then—she would have every last, bitter grain of it. 'But one night was not enough,' he declared. It had reminded him too acutely of what he had surrendered when he'd left England all those years before. But it had whetted his appetite too. He had suspected that it was too late for him and Alice, that not just some water, but a whole great ocean had flowed underneath their particular bridge—and yet he had wanted to savour every last drop of it before he said goodbye to her again.

How could he have anticipated that the Parisian trip would have flowed so easily—and that the solution had seemed to be staring right there at him in the face? Especially since time seemed to have quietened down Alice's own need for emotional reassurance.

'I never made any false promises to you, Alice,' he said.

Alice swallowed. Now he was twisting the knife so that the pain was becoming unendurable. But he was right, he hadn't. He hadn't told her that he loved her, or that he couldn't live without her. He had simply painted a picture of her own imagined future—a barren, withered future without the vital Greek by her side. He had implied that only a fool would turn down such an opportunity—but, really, only a fool would fall for it. And she had, hadn't she? Oh, yes, she had—hook, line and sinker.

But the picture was still not completely clear.

'What you mentioned earlier,' she said, frowning slightly in memory, 'about only having just bought it. What were you talking about?'

In the light of what else had happened, this now seemed of little consequence. 'I've recently completed a deal on Kalfera's bank. I've bought it,' he elaborated flatly, meeting her blank stare.

'You've bought a bank?' she repeated in disbelief.

'Yes, Alice. I own it—along with most of the real estate on the island.' He gave a short laugh. 'You want to know why I didn't tell you that either? Habit, I guess—it's become second nature to me to play down my wealth. It tends to attract the wrong kind of women.'

And oddly enough, this hurt almost as much as anything else he had told her. Didn't he realise that she'd loved him when he'd had nothing—did that *count* for nothing? 'You didn't trust me enough to tell me something like that?' she questioned slowly. 'Like I really would have cared about your money?'

'It was a misjudgement,' he said heavily.

'Too right it was, Kyros. One misjudgement too many.'

'But now that this is all out in the open,' he said

slowly, 'surely you can see the benefits of our marriage.'

'You mean our bizarre mockery of a marriage?'

He shook his dark head impatiently. 'Think about it, Alice—I mean, *really* think about it. Yes, I kept my fortune hidden from you—but by doing that you have proved that you did not marry me simply for my wealth.'

'You mean, I've passed some kind of test I didn't even know I was taking?' she demanded.

'That's being over-simplistic,' he argued. He smiled. 'Especially when you can now enjoy the benefits of that wealth.'

'I'm sorry?' she said, hoping and praying that he didn't mean what she thought he meant.

'I need a woman in my life,' he said deliberately. 'And you fulfil my needs more than anyone else.' His voice softened. 'You always did.'

'Am I supposed to fall over with gratitude at a rare compliment from the great Kyros Pavlidis?' she retorted, biting her lip to hold back the tears. 'And what's in it for me?' Apart from having a doomed attraction for a calculating man with stone for a heart.

'I'll tell you what's in it for you. You get to enjoy all the things that my wealth can provide for you,' he said. 'Every day can be like it was yesterday—remember how carefree you felt, how easy it was? I have a boat we can sail—a plane we can fly. We can island-hop on one of my helicopters.' His lips curved into a smile. 'Think about it—there will be no more scrimping and saving and making do—you shall have whatever you want, Alice.'

Except the thing which most eluded her—his love. But now she wasn't even sure she wanted that any more.

She stared at him, wanting to feel the great leap of excitement she felt whenever she normally looked at him. But she couldn't. Looking at him now was a whole new experience. He still came across as the Kyros she recognised, with those meltingly rugged features and black eyes darker than olives. And he still sounded like Kyros, with that deep, creamy voice underpinned with the sexy, lyrical accent. Physically, she still wanted him in a way she had never wanted another man.

But something had changed and she realised it was something in her. He *was* a stranger to her now—with his secret life and his secret fortune and his insulting offer, which basically boiled down to her giving him sex and him giving her money! He had had the cheek to turn up on her doorstep, complaining about her being dressed like a whore—whereas now he was treating her like one!

How different it had all been yesterday. How perfect it had felt—just as she'd imagined a honeymoon *should* feel. Only with the dawning of the new day she had learned the truth—that she had left her old life behind her to discover nothing but a *sham* in its place.

Oh, Alice, she thought. *Just what have you done?*

She looked up at him, still with that same flat feeling inside. 'And is that it? Are all the secrets out in the open now—or is there anything else you want to tell me?'

'No. Nothing more.' He thought she looked so insubstantial that a puff of wind might blow her away—if the air which surrounded them had not been so hot and still. His black gaze searched the almost transparent whiteness of her face and he turned away abruptly and went into the house, returning with a tray on which stood a bottle of iced water and a glass of what looked like brandy. 'Drink that,' he said.

'I don't want it.'

'Drink it—you've had a shock.'

'You don't say?' she questioned faintly, but she picked up the glass with fingers which were shaking and somehow managed to manoeuvre the glass to her lips. She took only a sip. It was brandy—but not as she knew it. This was Greek brandy—fiery and strong and, though it burned a certain comfort down into her stomach, it left behind a feeling of almost surreal calm.

Heavily, she put the glass down and stared at her toenails—all glittery bright and painted pink after a pre-wedding session at the beautician's. There might have been doubts in Alice's mind as she had sat in that scented salon back in England—but never in her wildest dreams could she have imagined this.

Kyros walked over to the balustrade and stared out at the blur of lemon trees, the glitter of water from the pool and the yet more glittering sea beyond, and then he turned back again to see that she hadn't moved. Sitting there as still and as silent as a statue, staring at her feet as if fascinated by them. 'Alice? For pity's sake—say something.'

Alice looked up and the cold, icy feeling in her heart made her feel very afraid. She couldn't stay here—she couldn't think straight. She needed to get away from his beautiful dark face and hard body— away from the scrutiny of those black eyes which, even now, were gleaming out the kind of appeal that a woman would find almost impossible to resist.

But resist it she must. Just as she needed to run from him, before he witnessed the breakdown which she suspected was imminent. She stood up. 'There's nothing *to* say. Don't you think we've said enough?'

He took a step towards her. 'Alice.'

But she closed her mind and her heart to the appeal in his black eyes. 'Don't touch me. Just leave me alone.'

He could tell that she meant it—and he watched as she lifted up her broad-brimmed hat with trembling fingers and crammed it down on her head so that her face was once more in shadow. 'Where are you going?' he demanded.

'Who knows? It's a secret!' she returned with biting

sarcasm and had the fleeting pleasure of seeing him wince before she turned and stormed off down the steps which led into the sunlit gardens.

CHAPTER NINE

ALICE didn't stop running until she was out of sight of the house—but her feet skidded to a halt on the dusty road as the blazing sun beat down on her. Fit as she was, the main town was miles away—and she didn't have a car, did she? In fact, she had very little—other than a suitcase full of summer clothes and her passport.

She couldn't face going down to the beach again, and so she went round to the other side of the gardens until she reached the swimming pool where earlier she had sat dangling her feet. But this time she found a seat shaded with blooms and she sank down onto it, at last giving into the flood of tears which had been threatening to spill ever since she had discovered the extent of Kyros's deception.

She was trapped.

She might be in the island home of a Greek billionaire with every conceivable luxury around her—but there was no way off the island without Kyros knowing and giving her permission to take off in his private plane or to sail away on his luxury yacht, which was no doubt sitting in the harbour. She remembered he'd told her there was a ferry which operated to the mainland several times a day—and she supposed that she could play the adventuress and catch that.

Except it landed at some port she'd never heard of, she didn't speak Greek—and the idea of trying to organise scheduled flights back to the UK filled her with dread. She didn't feel as if she even had the energy to pack her suitcase, let alone find her way back to England—all her strength and her spirit seemed to have evaporated beneath the blazing discomfort of her discovery.

And Alice was as trapped as surely as if she were locked in some kind of opulent prison cell.

Burying her face in her hands, she began to cry in a way she could never remember crying before—hot, salt tears washing away the dust of her crumbled dreams. She cried until there were no tears left, and her sobs had begun to quieten into shuddering breaths, and only then did she allow herself to consider which options lay open for her.

Rubbing at sore eyes, she stared down at the sea. There really were only two options, when you stopped to think about it. To go or to stay.

How could she possibly stay after this?

To spend her life with a man she couldn't trust would be unbearable. Yet the thought of going back filled her with an equal unease—for how could she bear to face anyone, to tell them what had happened here? Those looks of sympathy when she crept back— her brand-new wedding ring removed from her finger as if it had never been there. People would be either too embarrassed to mention it—the elephant in the sitting room—or they would want to probe her for every scandalous and painful detail.

And what would her parents say? How many variations of 'I told you so' were there? How could she hurt them, or worry them sick by going back in a state of high emotion—wouldn't it be better to return once she had accustomed herself to the harsh reality of what her marriage to Kyros had turned out to be?

Lost in thought, she sat and watched the sun move slowly across the sky until she realised she was really thirsty—and that she couldn't sit there for ever. She had to go and face up to the consequences of her discoveries.

She went straight to the kitchen—thankfully empty—where she drank two big glasses of water, which immediately made her feel better. She put the glass down noisily, expecting Kyros to appear—at least showing *some* signs of remorse—but he did not, and this only added to her temper.

Running upstairs, she locked herself in the bathroom and spent over an hour in there, shaving her legs and putting on a face pack and alternating her bitter unhappiness with a growing anger that Kyros was nowhere around for her to vent her rage on.

Didn't he care?

No, of course he didn't care—the cold-hearted brute! All he cared about were *his* needs—and it didn't matter how many of her feelings or sensibilities he trampled over in his attempt to get those needs met.

Knowing how much he hated trousers, she defiantly put on a pair in cool white linen, along with a black vest. Then she dried her hair and tied it up into the most complicated style she could manage. He liked her hair flowing down her back, did he? Well, let's see how he liked *this!*

But when she went back out into the bedroom, she almost jumped out of her skin—because there, on the window seat, sat Kyros. The noise of the shower meant she'd heard no one enter the room and somehow she had thought that he would stay away from the sanctum of their suite. She had been prepared to meet him downstairs, not here—not in the intimacy of their bedroom.

His black hair was ruffled and his olive skin glowed—as if he had been walking outside. He was wearing some light shirt which was open at the neck, his long legs encased in faded blue jeans—and there was not one shred of anything even resembling remorse on his handsome, sardonic face.

'So you're still here?' he mocked softly.

'What does it look like?' she answered furiously.

He thought she looked like a woman who was spoiling for a fight, and he felt the sudden kick of lust at his groin.

'I thought that after your dramatic exit you'd be halfway to England by now.'

'Well, that would be a very difficult thing to achieve, wouldn't it, Kyros? Since there's no way off the island without your magnanimous say-so! In effect, I'm stuck here because you control the airspace! Just as you seem to want to control everything else that you can lay your hands on—including me!'

'Are you trying to say you want to use my plane?' he questioned carelessly.

She wanted to slap him very hard across his arrogant cheek, but Alice wasn't foolish enough to go down that path. She knew Kyros well enough to sense that some of the tension which was tautening his powerful frame could be put down to desire. But it wasn't *her* he wanted—just sex. Anyone would do— she just happened to be the convenient wife who had legally been providing it!

'How can I possibly go back now?' she demanded.

He glanced at his watch. 'Well, the pilot will probably be having dinner soon, but I can get him to delay it if you're desperate—though tomorrow morning would be much better from a—'

'Please don't wilfully misunderstand me, Kyros,' she cut across him, even more furious now. Unless he really *did* care more about his pilot's stomach than the fact that his new wife had been humiliated and betrayed.

'And how am I doing that?' he questioned softly.

'I meant that I can't possibly go back to England,' she said. 'How can I when I've only been on honeymoon for two days? I've let out my apartment and I've handed my notice in at work. The career I worked so hard for lies in absolute ruins.' She shook her head. 'I remember my boss looking at me as if I was completely mad when she heard I was coming out to the middle of nowhere after such a whirlwind romance. How right she was!'

Now it made her want to weep when she thought about how casually she had let her old life go. She had been so certain that she wanted Kyros. So sure that he would give her what she wanted that she had been prepared to risk everything she'd worked so hard for.

Though when she stepped back to think about it—what else could she have done but marry him? There had been no other way to test out whether they had some kind of a future together. How could there have been, when he lived on a distant island and she was in West London? She had felt she knew Kyros because of their youthful romance—but now she realised that she didn't know him at all, and that maybe she never had.

Perhaps she should just admit to being a poor judge of character—or, rather, admit that she had spent too long viewing the world through rose-tinted glasses and it was about time she took them off, once and for all.

All along she had refused to accept Kyros as he really was—an arrogant, cold-hearted brute who had just wanted a convenient wife. Instead she had tried to mould him into what she wanted him to be. A loving and committed man.

But loving and committed men didn't turn up on your doorstep after ten years offering you a one-night stand, did they?

And women who wanted to be cherished and respected did not grab at the opportunity with both hands, did they?

'If I go back now, my parents will be worried sick,' she raged. 'I have no income and no place of my own—there's no way I can face moving in with them until my tenant moves out, and having to face their well-meaning recriminations.' Even worse would be their gentle expressions of sympathy—that her dreams had not worked out. To have to face *those* would break her heart. 'If I go back now I'm going to look like a total fool. I'll have to stay here—at least until the dust settles. People soon forget.'

For some reason her solution both offended and angered him. Was that her main concern—her damned reputation? 'So it is simply pride that keeps you in my home, is it, Alice?'

'Or self-respect,' she bit back.

'Which is a term women use to stop them doing

what they really want to do, in my experience,' he drawled.

'And we all know how extensive that is!'

'Some men might take that as a compliment, Alice.'

'I can assure you that it wasn't intended as one!'

He liked it when she was feisty—he liked it a little too much. The insistent clamour of desire began to skitter its way over his skin and he debated whether to go over there and subdue her in the way that women best liked to be subdued. But she certainly hadn't dressed like a woman who was sending out silent, sensual messages.

He thought how different she looked from yesterday—when she had shone and laughed so prettily in her glittery kaftan and a delicious swimsuit which had clung to every curve of her body. Yesterday, he had understood exactly why he had brought her back here wearing his ring.

Today her face was pale and her lips were trembling and her stunning hair was woven close to her head in a style which concealed one of her best features. She wore wide, mannish trousers which hid her beautiful legs and a cheap little vest which did her no favours at all. He was not stupid—he knew just why she had dressed like that. Her outfit was intended to punish him. Kyros's mouth curved into a cruel smile. Did she really think that by using clothes as a protective shield it would stop him desiring her? Or having her?

'Are you having dinner?' he questioned.

'I'm not hungry.'

He shrugged. 'Suit yourself. But please don't think you can start asking for trays of food to be sent up here as if you're some kind of invalid, because you're not.' His eyes flicked over her wide, trembling mouth. 'And starving yourself to make a point isn't going to win you any prizes.'

Alice watched in disbelief as he rose with panther-like grace from his window seat, and began to walk towards the door. That was *it?* End of discussion?

'And that's all you've got to say?'

'Oh, there's a hell of a lot more I'd like to say,' he said softly. 'But somehow I don't think that now is the right time.'

To Alice's fury, he left the room and after a couple of minutes she pulled the door open slightly to hear him talking to Sophia. And then the sound of music being put on—and the chink of cutlery and glass and a cork being popped. Later, she even heard the telephone ringing and Kyros's deep voice laughing as he spoke. Who the hell was he talking to who was making him laugh at this time of night?

Especially as she had effectively marooned herself up here!

She read five pages of the 'classic' novel she'd brought with her—and then forgot every word of it. And after that her stomach began to rumble alarmingly because it was hours since she'd eaten—but she was damned if she was going to lose face by creeping downstairs and asking for food. Or worse, to have to sit on the other side of the table from arrogant, secretive Kyros. Why, it would choke her.

She found an old packet of mints at the bottom of her suitcase and chewed on some of those, but all the time she was dreading when Kyros would reappear, dreading his reaction to what she was about to tell him.

He didn't appear until almost midnight, by which time Alice had fallen into shattered half-sleep—but she sat bolt upright up in bed once she heard the door open. He was yawning a little as he walked in—which she supposed was a good sign. Maybe this wasn't going to be as bad as she had anticipated.

'Kyros—we ought to discuss what we're going to do about sleeping arrangements.'

He snapped on one of the bedside lamps and turned to look at her. 'What's to discuss?' he questioned softly.

'Well, obviously—we can't both sleep…here.' She touched the space on the marital bed beside her rather as she might pat a poisonous snake as her mind played out scenes from last night's love-making with graphic and erotic recall.

He began to unbutton his shirt. 'Why not?'

'Because…' She wished he would stop undressing in front of her. 'You *know* why not, Kyros.'

'No, I don't, do tell me,' he drawled, his hand moving now to the zip of his jeans.

Alice swallowed. 'Because I don't want to have sex with you, that's why!'

'You're a liar, Alice,' he said softly. 'You want to have sex with me right now, don't you? In fact, I'm willing to bet that you're so turned on that I could come over there right now and take you without any preliminaries—just like I did on the floor of your apartment before we went to Paris—'

'You bastard!'

He shrugged. 'You knew that when you married me. If you didn't want that then you should have married a nice guy, shouldn't you?'

Infuriatingly, she felt wrong-footed—because there really was no logical argument to that one. 'Anyway, I've...I've made up the daybed,' she said, pointing to the sheets which she'd carefully tucked in, the two pillows and coverlet she'd found in the linen closet. She glossed him a hopeful smile. 'It's quite comfortable, really. You can sleep there, can't you, Kyros?'

The jeans slid down and he hung them over the back of a chair, along with his boxer shorts. 'No.'

Alice opened her mouth to reason with him, but she could see from the dark look of determination on his face that he would not be reasoned with. And he was naked, too—dangerously naked, because Kyros didn't seem to have a state of being which didn't involve some kind of arousal.

'Then I suppose I'll have to sleep there myself!' she snapped.

'You think so?'

'I don't have a choice, do I, Kyros?' she questioned as she climbed out of bed.

She got as far as halfway across the room in her baggiest T-shirt and least skimpy pair of knickers. Kirsty had given her a gorgeous pale green silk nightdress as a wedding present—but she wasn't going to give Kyros the wrong idea by wearing *that* as a cover-up. But frankly, from the sudden hardening of his mouth and the fiery glint from his eyes, he seemed to be getting the wrong idea anyway, because his hand had snaked out to catch hold of her—and before she knew it he had brought her up close to him.

'Where do you think you're going, Alice *mou?*'

'Let…let go of me,' she breathed.

'Where do you think you're going?' he repeated softly.

'If you won't sleep on the daybed—then I'll have to!'

'But that is where you are completely wrong, *agape mou.*'

Trying to ignore his nakedness and his very obvious growing arousal, Alice set her face into an expression of outrage. 'Are you trying to tell me you're *forbidding* me to sleep where I want, Kyros?'

He smiled. 'Damned right I am,' he assented silkily, his fingers splaying arrogantly around her tiny waist. 'You agreed to marry me—and as long as you stay under my roof you will fulfil your obligations as a wife!'

Alice felt faint with disbelief, and with something else far more dangerous. 'Wh…what are you talking about?'

'Oh, come on—you're an intelligent woman, Alice,' he mocked as he brought her even closer. 'You know exactly what I'm talking about. Or maybe you fall into that category of woman who likes to be shown, rather than told.'

He could not have insulted her more if he'd tried. Somehow he'd managed to make her sound like just one of a long line of tame females who had graced his bed—as if their marriage had counted for nothing at all!

'But this is the twenty-first century!' she protested as he gave a low, devilish laugh. 'You can't treat women like this!'

'Twenty-first century woman be damned! That's just the superficial top layer—deep down women haven't changed since the beginning of time. They want a man who is strong and hard, who will make love to them until they cry out.'

In his arms, Alice struggled—more because she felt she ought to than because she really wanted to— and the ineffectual movement had the undesirable effect of wriggling her against the unmistakable power of his erection.

She looked straight into his eyes as her heart raced. 'You…'

'You can call me all the names under the sun but I know what you want, Alice *mou*—and now I'm going to give it to you,' he vowed softly as he caught her in his arms and plundered her mouth with his own.

Alice's last sane thought was that anger must be the biggest aphrodisiac in the world, because never had she felt it coursing so insistently around her veins as she did at that moment—and never had she been quite so turned on.

She gasped when he peeled off her T-shirt and pressed her swollen breasts against his chest with a little groan of delight, and she gasped again when he ripped off her knickers—though the sound was not one of objection, but of entreaty. Because he was right—she *wanted* this. Or rather, she wanted *him*—she wanted Kyros's love and heart and devotion—and maybe this was all she was going to get.

He picked her up and carried her over to the bed as she had known he would, like a victor with his spoils, and he set her down on the feathery mattress, his face a series of shifting shadows as he towered over her for a moment.

'Let's get one thing clear, shall we? While you're in my house, you sleep in my bed—is that understood, Alice?'

'Yes,' she whispered. Yes, yes, yes. And then her arms went up around his neck to pull him down to her.

CHAPTER TEN

ALICE woke up the following morning scarcely able to believe what had happened. Or rather, what she had done.

She lay there with her eyes still closed, feeling exhausted—both physically and emotionally. She felt as if Kyros had taken from her everything which was hers to give—stealing her resolve and determination and replacing them with a series of sensual delights. Yet he had not been alone in his demands—for Alice could never remember behaving quite as uninhibitedly as she had last night.

It was as if her sense of injustice at the way he had lied to her had liberated her completely. She was no longer seeking his approval—not in anything—and her sensual demands had for once exceeded even his. At one point, Kyros had flopped back against the soft bank of pillows, blinking up at the ceiling in semi-disbelief.

'Maybe I should make you angry a little more often

if this is how I am to be rewarded, *agape mou,*' he murmured, a smile of satisfaction playing at the edges of his mouth.

Alice could have wept—or hit him—but what did she expect? She had fallen into his arms and under his spell with almost insulting ease—it had taken no more than one savagely passionate kiss and she had capitulated. If he wasn't treating her like a delicate little flower to be cherished, she had only herself to blame.

Slowly, she opened her eyes to see him standing naked in front of the open windows as glorious sunlight flooded over his body and into the room. Beyond his silhouetted figure she could see the dazzling sapphire of the sea and, above that, the bright blue of the sky. As honeymoon destinations went, you didn't get much better than this—and this was actually Kyros's *home!* It should have been perfect—except that she felt like a jigsaw with a vital, heart-shaped piece missing.

She studied him. Viewed naked from behind, he looked like one of those flawless marble statues you saw in museums—honed masculinity in its most faultless form. His shoulders were broad, tapering down through narrow hips to the firm, hard swell of his buttocks and the muscular shafts of his powerful legs. There were faint, pale marks where he must have worn swimming trunks and Alice foolishly found herself yearning for another golden day like the day before yesterday, when he had sat watching her swim—and all had seemed so right with the world.

He turned round, his black eyes glittering, and he gave a sigh of satisfaction as he stared at the pale blonde hair where it lay like tangled silk across the pillow. 'So you are awake, my beauty.'

'Obviously.'

He laughed. 'Now, now—do not be sour, sweet Alice. I would have thought that all the pleasure I'd given you last night would have put you in a sunny mood this morning.'

'Then you were wrong if you think that…that…'

'That what, *glyka mou?*' he questioned softly.

She averted her eyes. 'That a bout of sex makes everything better.'

Kyros eyed her thoughtfully, but inside he felt a sense of frustration. Was she so crazy that she failed to see what was in front of her nose—that the chemistry between them was extraordinary? And so stubborn that she was prepared to continue a war of words simply because life did not fit her idealistic vision of it? He had thought that she had transcended all that emotional neediness—hadn't that been one of his reasons for asking her to marry him?

He walked over towards the bed, seeing her gaze drawn inexorably towards the cradle of his groin, where the hard heat of desire was unfurling itself—despite her best attempts to look away.

'What…what do you think you're doing?' she

questioned in alarm as he leaned over her, smelling of toothpaste and soap, all mixed up with the unmistakable scent of arousal.

'I am about to kiss you good morning.'

She turned her head sideways. 'Well, don't.'

'No?' His lips grazed her neck.

'No.'

'Sure?'

'Kyros—'

'Shh.' He pulled back the duvet from her unresisting fingers and climbed into bed beside her. 'Stop fighting it, Alice—stop fighting yourself. You know you want me.'

She opened her mouth to deny it, but the falsehood was never uttered because Kyros began a swift but extremely efficient seduction, which almost ended with her blurting out that she loved him, but somehow she bit it back—because she didn't. She definitely didn't.

Afterwards, she turned her back on him.

His finger played with a long strand of hair which had attached itself to her damp back. 'What's the matter, Alice?' he questioned softly. 'You are angry with me? Or with yourself?'

'No, I'm tired, that's all.' But she couldn't bear to see the look of satisfaction written all over his darkly handsome face. If there had been a battle of wills last night and again just now—then Kyros was the unchallenged winner.

'Then go back to sleep,' he said softly. 'There's no

need for you to get up. I'm going to spend the day at the bank—there's still some paperwork I need to see to.' He let his hand rest lightly on her hip, his thumb rubbing reflectively at the slight jut of the bone which lay just below the surface of her silken skin. 'And don't go on some self-imposed starvation campaign, *agape mou*. I don't want you fading away before my eyes.'

Alice didn't answer. She feigned sleep while he dressed and even managed to perpetuate it when he came back over to the bed.

Kyros stared down at her. Did she really think she was fooling him into thinking that she was asleep? No more than she had managed to keep up the pretence of not desiring him. Wasn't she aware that there were a million ways you could read a woman's body language—and hers was positively shrieking to him that she found him irresistible? She always had.

'*Herete,* Alice,' he whispered.

Once she was certain that he'd left, Alice showered and dressed and went downstairs—checking to make sure that his racy car had gone, but it had. Only Sophia's rather battered old car was sitting on the drive.

She ate breakfast on the terrace, dribbling a thick amber spoonful of Kalfera honey over a hunk of deliciously crusty bread.

'You are very hungry this morning,' observed Sophia.

Alice's cheeks flushed pink. 'Er, yes. I missed dinner last night.'

It was an odd sort of day, mainly because she felt so displaced—she didn't feel like a wife and yet she no longer felt single. Kalfera wasn't home—and yet, despite all the luxurious comforts on tap, it didn't feel like being on holiday either.

But it wasn't difficult to pretend she was—she would have defied anyone not to have been transfixed by the beauty of the villa and its views. She spent several enjoyable hours sunbathing, swimming and reading her book. She swam fifty lengths of the pool and afterwards ate olives and salad for lunch. And once the heat had gone out of the afternoon sun, she even went off on a walk up a narrow mountain track— where she saw some sweet-looking goats grazing on the rather arid-looking grass.

As the day wore on she could feel some of the tension seeping away from her, dissolved by the sun and the warm, fragrant air. She was horribly aware of her mind playing tricks on her by reminding her how wonderful the previous night had been—as if it was trying to make her forget the bitter row which had gone before.

Could they work something out? she found herself wondering with a sudden pang of longing. Some kind of compromise? Couldn't Kyros see for himself that being tender and passionate in bed was only a short step away from allowing those feelings to spill over into the rest of his life?

Like admitting he loves you? mocked a voice inside her head. *You never give up, do you, Alice?*

By six, Kyros still wasn't back, and after changing for dinner Alice decided to explore the downstairs of the house properly—if only to get her bearings. There seemed to be several large rooms which could be used for sitting in, or entertaining. There was a grand piano in one, and row upon row of books in another—all in Greek, she noted. And a distinct lack of photographs—she couldn't find one anywhere even though she hunted on all the shelves.

'What do you think you're doing?'

Alice spun round to find Kyros standing in the doorway watching her—his cold expression a whole world away from the man who had tangled her hair in his fingers this morning and pulled her down to kiss him again.

'Just looking.'

'Looking for something in particular?' He removed his linen jacket.

Would it sound as if she were weakening her position if she told him that she wanted to find out more about what made him tick? 'I couldn't help noticing that there aren't any photos anywhere.'

There was a pause. 'What kind of photos were you expecting to see, Alice?'

'Well, some of Olympia, at least.'

'But Olympia doesn't live here,' he informed her coolly.

'No, I know that—but you *are* her father.'

'Yes,' he continued. 'I am. And as such I will decide whether or not I want photos of her around.'

Alice drew a deep breath, ignoring the dark note in his voice. 'There are none of your twin brother either—do you realise I've never even seen a picture of him? I mean, I suppose he must look exactly the same as you—but it would be nice.'

'Alice,' he said warningly. 'This is none of your business.'

'Or your father,' she said. 'Or—'

'Don't!' The word cut across her like an icy whip before she could say it. 'Don't pry into my life, Alice—do you understand me?'

But Alice clutched at his fury as if it were a lifeline. 'Why do you never talk about anything?' she demanded. 'About what happened in your past? About what it makes you feel?'

'Because the facts don't change and everything else is superfluous,' he iced out. 'And I certainly don't intend talking about them in order to satisfy your curiosity.'

It was as if he had slammed a door shut in her face and she stared at him. 'That's an *unbearable* thing to say,' she whispered.

'You think so?' Angry now, he tensed. 'Then why do you stay?'

Biting her lip, she turned away. 'You know why. Because I can't go back—not yet. It's too soon.'

'But that's not the whole story, is it?' he challenged softly, catching hold of her and pulling her round into his arms. 'You don't want to go back because you can't bear to leave me, can you, Alice? Because you find me utterly irresistible. Because when I take you in my arms...like this...'

His touch was like electricity. 'That's...that's not fair,' she whispered.

'Life isn't fair, *agape mou*—have you only just realised that?'

She wanted to weep at his cold-blooded manipulation—but not for long, because soon he was kissing away every last doubt. And although physically he made her feel so defenceless, she found he was right—she really could not resist him.

'See how much better things can be when you just accept them for what they are?' he murmured against her lips. 'Do you want to keep fighting me and stirring things up, Alice?'

Mutely, she shook her head as he locked the door and began to kiss her.

'Isn't this better? Mmm?'

It was short, perfunctory—physically satisfying and emotionally empty—and afterwards he adjusted his clothing and picked up his jacket with the same kind of detachment as if he had just eaten a meal. It was just that a different appetite had been satisfied,

Alice thought bitterly. But having sex with Kyros was a bit like having fast food—after an hour when the glow had worn off she was left aching with all her insecurities.

'Are you eating with me tonight?' he queried.

Pride could be a lonely companion—and what good would sitting alone in a room do? Slowly, she nodded her head. 'Yes, Kyros—I'll be eating with you.'

'Good.' He paused as he unlocked the door. 'I'll go and let Sophia know.'

The meal had been laid in the beautiful dining room. Tall candles flickered over the crystal glasses and silver cutlery and the room was scented with the heady fragrance of vases filled with tiny white flowers.

Kyros put his wineglass down and studied her. 'I spoke to Olympia today. She wants to come over here.'

'For tea?' remembered Alice.

His lips curved into a half-smile. 'Something like that. She wants to bring her aunt Eleni with her.'

'Katarina's sister? Who I presume wants to give your wife the once-over?'

Their eyes met in a long moment. 'You know your own sex better than I do.'

In spite of everything, Alice laughed. 'Oh, I doubt that, Kyros. When are they coming?'

'I thought we could have them here tomorrow. Would you like that?'

How like a real married couple they sounded, she

thought, with a pang, sipping at the rich red wine and hoping that it might dull the ache in her heart before her cold, sexy husband took her to bed and broke it once more.

But Alice found she was excited about seeing Olympia again. In a funny sort of way she identified with the little girl and her sense of not quite belonging—and, of course, she was curious to meet Eleni. Would Eleni resent the Englishwoman who had married her dead sister's fiancé? Or would she guess that beneath the surface all was not as it seemed?

In the event, she needn't have worried. Eleni was so caught up in the excitement of her own marriage that she barely seemed to notice that Kyros and Alice weren't playing the textbook version of newly-weds with extravagant displays of emotion.

And Olympia was so sweet. 'Can we swim?' she asked eagerly.

'Of course you can,' said Kyros.

'You swim with me, Papa!'

He shook his head. 'I must make a few calls while you're in the pool, *pedhi mou*,' he demurred. 'I'll watch you from the side.'

Don't judge, thought Alice, balling her fingers into little fists. *It's none of your business if he puts his business before playing with his little girl.*

'I want someone to play with,' pouted Olympia.

Eleni was shaking her head. 'And don't look at me,

pedhi,' she said. 'I'm going out later—and I don't want to mess up my hair.'

'I'll come in with you, Olympia,' said Alice suddenly.

The little girl's face lit up. '*Will* you?'

'Of course I will!'

Alice pulled off her kaftan and dived into the pool. In a way, it was great to be away from the adults and her fears—wondering what sort of impression she was making on Eleni and trying not to act awkwardly with Kyros. And Olympia was a lovely little girl. She'd had a rough entry into the world, thought Alice. Losing her mother when she was a little baby and only seeing her father from a distance was a terrible way to start her life. How unlike her own settled and secure upbringing, with two parents who were still together.

Without wanting to, she found herself thinking about what it must have been like when Kyros's mother had left. On a small island like this, everyone must have heard about it almost straight away—not like in England. When family break-ups had happened to friends of hers, they had managed to stave off telling people until the initial pain had faded. So that they'd been able to come to school with a bright face and say they didn't really care, and only the most discerning eye would detect the tell-tale wobble in the voice which stated very clearly that they *did.*

Had Kyros done the proud thing too, to fend off unwanted sympathy? she wondered. Stealing a glance at the hard, handsome face—his expression unreadable behind the dark glasses he wore—she suspected that he had.

'Can you do the butterfly stroke?' asked Olympia.

Alice turned round and grinned. 'I can try!'

It was exhausting and exhilarating splashing through the water with a lively five-year-old and for a while Alice forgot about everything except having fun.

Ignoring the insistent buzz of his phone, Kyros sat and watched her—but for once his focus was not her sleek body as she twisted through the water like an eel and then scooped up the laughing child in her arms. She seemed oblivious to the world as they splashed water over each other—Alice's hair soaking wet and plastered to her head like seaweed.

'Your phone keeps ringing.' Eleni's voice broke into his thoughts.

Behind his dark shades, Kyros's eyes narrowed—and then, with a slight click of irritation, he pulled the phone from his pocket and turned it off.

Eleni pulled a face of mock-shock. 'I don't believe it! Are you feeling okay?' she joked, and then added, in Greek, 'She is lovely, Kyros.'

'Yes.' He said nothing more. He liked Eleni well enough, but was aware that anything he said would be repeated and Kyros had no desire for his life to be dissected by others. Hadn't he had enough of that to last a lifetime?

Lifting a now-shivering Olympia out and directing her towards a towel, Alice rested her arms on the side. 'Isn't anyone else coming in?'

He thought how her wet eyelashes made her eyes look like stars and he thought how impossible it would be for him to be in a swimming pool with her with people looking on…

He switched his phone back on. 'I have a couple of calls to make,' he said.

And Alice slipped back beneath the turquoise water before anyone could see that her eyes were wet with tears.

CHAPTER ELEVEN

'AND you are sure you do not mind, Alice?'

'No, I'm positive—and really happy to help,' said Alice, switching the receiver from one ear to another. 'From two until four, you say? No, that's fine—I'll see you both later. Bye, Eleni.'

She put the phone down just as Kyros came downstairs carrying an overnight bag—and she lifted her face to meet his blistering black scrutiny.

'What was that all about?' he demanded.

Alice smoothed her hair back. 'I said I'd take Olympia to a party on the other side of the island this afternoon.'

'You?' He put the bag down and frowned—for something about Alice forging a relationship with his daughter made him feel distinctly uneasy. 'Why can't Eleni take her?'

'Because she and her mother want to go shopping for wedding dresses on the mainland,' said Alice, and then hesitated. He took so much for granted.

She wanted to remind him that Eleni wasn't Olympia's mother and that soon she would probably have children of her own, and had he thought about what would happen then? But he was due to fly to Rome on business and was staying over—and this would be the first time he had left her on the island or been away for a night, and...

And what? Was she hoping that he was going to discover he missed her—that he might return from Italy a different man? If only people behaved how we wanted them to behave, thought Alice ruefully. She wasn't expecting undying love from him—even if she couldn't stop herself from hoping for just a little—all she wanted was for Kyros to just be a little less uptight outside the bedroom.

'And just how are you proposing to get her there?' he queried.

Alice frowned as his curt question cut into her thoughts. 'By car, of course.'

'Of *course?*' he echoed sarcastically. 'You mean my car, since you don't have one?'

Wasn't his car also supposed to be her car, since they were married? 'Well, yes—if you want to do a big male possessive thing about it—but I can't really think why you'd object to me borrowing it.'

'Because it's a powerful car, Alice,' he said damn-ingly. 'Do you really think you'll be able to handle it?'

Alice bit back her anger as she looked at him. How hard it was to reconcile this granite-faced man with the passionate lover in whose arms she had lain earlier. Against whom she had softly sighed her contentment as he'd wrapped his body around hers as if he couldn't bear to let her go—and wasn't it that kind of behaviour which kept all her stupid hopes alive? As if by sleeping with him, she might finally break through all the emotional barriers he had built up?

Well, one look at his flinty expression as he made disparaging comments about her ability to drive should help drive the message home that she was mistaken.

'Do you want to take Olympia to the party, then?' she demanded.

'How can I—when I have to be in Italy on business?'

'Exactly!' Alice rounded on him, her patience finally snapping after all the days and hours and minutes of veering between grand passion and walking on eggshells—because his mightiness couldn't bear to hear anything that resembled real life. Well, he would damned well hear it now!

'*You* can't take her—and yet you don't want me to take her. What's the matter, Kyros? Are you afraid of someone else getting close to your daughter even if you can't bear the thought of doing that yourself?'

'That's enough!' he gritted out.

'No.' Alice sucked in a deep and ragged breath. 'It is *not* enough. It's about time you heard a few home truths and since no one else seems able to stand up to you, then maybe it should be from me. Because you're a coward, Kyros—nothing but a coward.'

There was a deathly hush.

'You dare to call *me* a *coward?*'

'Yes, I do—and I mean every word of it. An emotional coward—and it's doing you nothing but *harm.*' Her voice caught alive with passion now and suddenly the words were tumbling out—as if they were in a hurry to escape from her mouth after having been bitten back for so long.

'You keep everyone at arm's length because you can't bear the thought of being hurt again, like you were when your mother left. But your attitude is making history repeat itself, Kyros. You can't see what you've got—because you certainly don't appreciate it. A daughter who's dying to love you and a wife—'

'A wife who doesn't know when to keep her mouth shut!'

Alice fell silent, shaking her head in resignation as she stared at the fury etched on his dark features. What was the use? He wouldn't listen—he never did. That wall he'd built around himself was so high that nobody would ever be able to knock it down—had she really thought that she was in with a chance?

'So what are we going to do about the car?' she questioned quietly. 'I managed to pass my driving test first time—and I don't have a single point on my licence. But if you, in your infinite and unquestionable wisdom, don't think I'm fit to drive your powerful machine, then I'll get a taxi. Or I'll borrow Sophia's.'

'You are not being seen out in *that,*' he snapped.

Stonily, she stared at him as she held out her hand. 'In that case—may I please have the keys?'

There was a long silence while he tussled with himself to say something to respond to her outrageous tirade against him—but no words seemed to come and, with something like a snarl, he handed the keys over.

He was forced to order himself a taxi to take him to the airport—something he had not done for as long as he could remember—and he was still simmering with rage as the plane took off. Staring down out of the window, he could see the huge sapphire basin of the sea, flecked with tiny little white waves, but he barely noticed the little boats bobbing around.

Just who did she think she was, speaking to him in such a discourteous way of things which were none of her business?

She's your wife, prompted a little voice in his head. *And that is what wives do.*

Well, he did not want a wife who did not know her place!

Impatiently, he shook his head as the stewardess offered him a drink. He would not tolerate Alice's interference—he would not.

But somehow she had planted the seeds of discontent in his mind. Some of her words had unexpectedly hit home and, although at first he tried to tell himself that she did not know what she was talking about, his thoughts gave way to an uncomfortable reflection.

He was unable to concentrate on the paperwork he had brought with him—or on his meeting at a glitzy office in Italy's capital. He was due to have a late lunch with someone from the Greek Embassy, but at the last minute Kyros cancelled—citing family reasons.

He called his pilot. 'I want to return to Kalfera,' he said.

'Today, *kyrio?*' asked the pilot in surprise.

'Yes, today. As soon as possible.'

His flight touched down in Kalfera in the blistering heat of the late afternoon and the pilot had already radioed ahead to have a taxi waiting. All the way back, Kyros's thoughts had been swarming around in his head until at last he began to reluctantly concede that maybe Alice had a point. Maybe it *was* time to make a more regular arrangement to see Olympia.

It was just past five by the time he returned home but the villa was open and his car was nowhere to be seen. He frowned slightly as he walked into the house and Sophia came running out, looking flustered.

'We were not expecting you back, *kyrio*—'

'Alice and Olympia have not returned?'

'No, *kyrio*—I think they are still at the party.'

He glanced at his watch and frowned. 'When my

wife brings Olympia back—then please give me a shout.'

'Yes, *kyrio.*'

He went to his study to work—but the minutes ticked by and still Alice did not appear. Sophia left for the evening and irritation gave way to concern and then anger when he looked at his watch to see that it was now past seven.

Where the hell was she?

He went outside to the front of the villa to scan the road, but there was no sign of his zippy little sports car approaching and he felt the first real hammer of fear.

He had told her not to drive it and he had told her it was too powerful! And she—stubborn, stubborn Alice—had refused to listen to him. She had turned his concern for her ability to handle such a powerful machine into a sexist rant—and then an attack on the way he chose to bring his daughter up.

How dared she? How *dared* she?

He paced the gravel drive while his mind conjured up images of mangled metal and…and… With a low, almost feral growl of pain he reached in his pocket for his phone, intending to call the police chief, when at that moment he heard the familiar but distant drone of a car and Kyros stilled.

For there, buzzing up the road in his car like a little silver fly, was Alice—her blonde hair tied back, and as she approached he could see a look of carefree enjoyment on her face as the wind whipped at it.

He barely constrained himself until she had turned off the engine and then he ran to the door and wrenched it open. 'Where is Olympia?' he snapped.

So his foul mood of this morning had not dissipated, Alice thought. 'I dropped her back home.'

He felt his breath escape him in a long hiss. 'Where the hell have you been?' he demanded.

'I took her to a party, you knew that—'

'The party finished at *four!*' he exploded. 'And it is now gone seven. And so I ask you again, Alice—where have you been?'

She tried to tell herself that it was worry about his daughter making him react like this—but somehow she couldn't quite believe it. He didn't act like the textbook father the rest of the time, did he? No, this was just more of the same—Kyros treating people like possessions, wanting to pick them up and then put them down whenever it suited him. A daughter to be brought out like a doll from a box whenever he could be bothered—and a wife who was good for sex and not much else, as far as she could make out.

She jumped out of the car and turned to face him. 'It was a gorgeous afternoon—and so we found a lovely little beach and went swimming and made sandcastles after the party finished. Why shouldn't we? It's not a crime to play with a child, Kyros—although clearly you think it is. We had already told her grandparents that we might be late. Did you check with them?'

'I didn't want to worry them,' he retorted.

'No?' Alice shook her head. 'I don't know whether I believe you. Probably you couldn't bear for them or anyone else to think you weren't running the entire show—as usual. The bloody director—but one who keeps everyone at arm's length!'

'That's quite enough!'

She clenched her fists by her sides and suddenly she knew that she could no longer keep on battling the inevitable. 'Too right it is—more than enough! I'm out of here, Kyros. Do you understand? I'm leaving—I can't live with you any more. I was crazy to think that you might ever change. That you might ever start behaving like a human being with a heart and with... with *feelings* that you wouldn't mind expressing now and again, like real married couples do.' She shook her head. 'Who cares about pride? I'll swallow mine and go home and face all the mocking faces—because anything has to be better than living with a damned robot!'

She steadied her breathing with an effort, looking into his disbelieving face but feeling quite calm now that she had come to a decision. 'So I'd like you to arrange for the plane to fly me out of here tonight, please—and to call me a taxi. And now I'm going upstairs to pack.'

CHAPTER TWELVE

KYROS told himself that she did not mean it. Alice would not go. She would realise that they had both said a lot of hotheaded things in the spur of the moment—but that was all.

He waited downstairs for her to reappear, her eyes red from crying—telling him she'd made a big mistake.

But she did not come—and the distant sound of drawers and doors being opened and closed told him that she might actually be packing her suitcase ready to fly back to England.

Well, let her leave, then. Let her! He did not need her. Furiously, Kyros picked up the phone, ordered a taxi and put his plane on stand-by and he was in his study when she finally came downstairs and he heard the sound of a suitcase being placed heavily on the floor of the hall.

'Kyros?' she called.

He took a moment or two before he walked out, his

heart beating very hard. She was very pale, and there was a strange, set look to her mouth. He raised his eyebrows at her in silent query.

'I've come to say goodbye,' she said.

They stared at one another until the sound of a horn beeping outside shattered the silence.

'There's your taxi,' he said at last.

Alice stared at him. Was that it? The kiss she had been both fearing and longing for had not material-ised—and neither, it seemed, did any words of regret.

'I'll bring your case,' he said, and picked it up.

Keep your nerve, she told herself. *Don't lose it now, because that's the trouble with being a convenient wife—you can be disposed of as simply as this. Just like this.*

The driver leapt out and put the case in the boot and Alice got into the back seat without another word. Only when the driver began to press on the accelera-tor did she turn her head and Kyros thought that her emerald eyes looked unnaturally bright.

'Give...give my love to Olympia,' she said. 'Tell her I'll send her a postcard.'

And then the taxi was gone in a cloud of dust, clunking its way down the mountain road towards the airstrip.

Damn her, thought Kyros as he went inside and poured himself a drink. He was better off without a woman who meddled—who wanted more than he was ever prepared to give.

But the drink lay untasted and a slow simmering of disquiet began to bubble away inside him as he tried to work out what it was that felt so wrong. And then he realised.

It was the silence.

There was no sense of Alice being in another room. No certainty that when he looked up he would be confronted with her particular golden and pink beauty. Memories began to pour into his mind like honey. Her sweetness with Olympia, yet the stern way she had alerted him to the fact that he was not giving his daughter what a father should—how fearless she could be. That way she had of biting her lip before she was about to laugh. The scent and feel of her body in his bed at night. Every night.

She was gone. Back on a plane to start her life over again in England—and he would never see her again because he had blown it. He had driven her away with his coldness and his cruelty and his manipulative use of sexual mastery.

And Kyros suddenly realised what he had done in his arrogance and short-sightedness. He had risked losing the two people he loved more than anything on earth—all in some vain attempt to try to shield himself from the stuff of life. And Alice had had the courage to tell him as few others would have done—to face the wrath of his rage and actually spell it out.

He had to stop her.

He glanced at his watch. It might be too late. The

taxi might have been faster than usual—and the pilot had been told to commence take-off as soon as she arrived. He punched out a telephone number to the control tower, but the line was busy, and he realised that he could waste the next twenty minutes trying to get through—or he could take action.

Kyros jumped to his feet and grabbed his car keys, ran outside and leapt into the sports car—accelerating off with a squeal of tyres. The road was winding with plenty of hairpin bends and a precipitous drop to one side—but Kyros knew that road as well as he knew the lines on his palm and he drove as fast as was safe.

The stars were beginning to appear in the sky as he raced towards the small airstrip—with its one control tower twinkling a green light from its summit.

The plane was still there—but only just. The mighty roar of the powerful engines filled his ears and as he watched he could see the sudden whirling of the propellers growing ever faster. And Kyros knew that he did not have a second to waste. A figure in the tower was signalling to him, but he ignored it as he drove his car straight onto the airstrip—screeching right in front of the startled pilot's line of vision.

Jumping out of the car, he began waving his arms frantically and suddenly the sound of the engines lessened and the propeller speed began to decrease. From out of one of the porthole windows he could see Alice's pale and disbelieving face, but then the steps were being lowered and he ran up them—faster than he had run in years.

He appeared inside the cabin, his breathing rapid and laboured, but Alice hadn't moved—she just sat there in her seat, as pale and still as if she had been turned to stone.

'Alice,' he said—and suddenly he did not care if the pilot could hear, or if she would be immovable on this. She might have decided that she did not want him no matter what he said, but he knew that he had to take that risk. 'Alice, don't go.'

Be strong, she told herself. *Be strong.* 'I have to go,' she said, and then repeated it as if trying to drum it in. 'I have to.'

He came forward and crouched down so that their eyes were on a level. Black blazing into green. 'Even if I told you I love you?'

Her mouth wobbled—because he didn't mean it. How could he? 'No, you don't,' she whispered.

He nodded. 'I thought about all the things you said. Things which hurt—but things which were true. I *haven't* been a good father to Olympia—not a bad one, just not close, or consistent enough. And I've been an absolutely terrible husband to you. I haven't allowed myself to love you—as you deserve to be loved.' He picked up her right hand in his and studied it, noting that the shiny new wedding band still lay firmly in place. Was that a sign that she might have reserved a corner of forgiveness in her heart—a beacon of light shimmering in a landscape which would be as dark as a starless night if she left him?

'I love you,' he said, when still she did not speak. 'I love you, Alice. More than that I cannot say—for I do not know the words.'

And Alice's heart missed a beat. Because this was Kyros as vulnerable and as open as she had ever seen him—admitting, probably for the first time in his life, a kind of human frailty. It was true—he did not know the words for love, or how to express it. But then how could he, for who had ever shown Kyros?

But he had told her he loved her—and he was a man who would never squander words like that. Didn't his declaration give her the freedom to begin the greatest adventure of her life, something she had wanted for so long—the freedom to love him back and to teach him how to love?

'Oh, Kyros,' she said brokenly. 'Kyros.'

He took her other hand in his. 'Why are you cry-ing?' he demanded fiercely. 'Tell me that, Alice?'

She shook her head. 'Darling, darling Kyros—I'm crying because I'm happy, that's all.'

Now he was dazed—and confused—but a sense of deep peace began to lap at the edges of his heart and he kissed each of her fingertips in turn. 'Will you come home with me now?' he asked simply.

She flung her arms around his neck and whispered in his ear as the last of the tears slipped down her cheeks. 'Oh, yes, my darling—I'll come home.'

EPILOGUE

Two glasses were chinked together and the two men drank a toast as their wives looked on—seemingly oblivious to the fact that almost everyone in the up-market New York restaurant was watching them from out of the corners of their eyes.

But then the two men were a remarkable pair, thought Alice—they drew the eye like magnets. Both so tall and lean, with their jet-dark eyes and hard, handsome faces. Individually, they would have turned heads—but multiply all that sensual masculinity by two and you had two identical men. Identical twins who were putting years of feuding and misunderstanding behind them to forge a new relationship.

Well, people *said* they were identical...

Alice turned to Xandros's wife. 'Can you tell them apart?' she asked.

Rebecca smiled. 'Oh, yes.'

'Me, too. I don't know how...I think it's something in the way that Kyros smiles that's so different.'

And Alice sighed, because he smiled so much these days—but then, as he was always telling her, there was plenty to smile about. It was as if, by coming so close to losing her, he had begun to be grateful for what he had. To appreciate his good fortune for the first time in his life.

He and Alice had been spending the week in New York, visiting Xandros and his family. Alice adored her brother and sister-in-law—and their wonderful house in Gramercy Park—and she had fallen completely in love with Xandros and Rebecca's cute little twin baby boys.

Kyros had watched her as she'd cradled little Andreas and his eyes had softened with understanding. 'Would you like to have my baby, Alice *mou?*'

She had been thinking about it all week, as, she suspected, had he. 'Oh, yes, please,' she had whispered. 'Just not yet. First I want you all to myself, my darling Kyros. And so does Olympia.'

Because Olympia now had a place in their home as well as in Kyros's heart—a place that was growing all the time. But that was love for you, thought Alice—if you gave it enough room, the potential was never-ending. They had promised to bring Olympia out here at Christmas time and Alice had already sent her a postcard.

'It's sooo snowy here at Christmas,' she had written. 'And Uncle Xandros says you'll be able to go skating in Central Park.'

She felt a warm glow inside her as she stirred her coffee, but Kyros and Xandros had started speaking in Greek and were now ordering another round of drinks.

Alice frowned as the two men lifted a cloudy mouthful to their lips. 'What are they drinking?' she whispered to Rebecca.

'Ouzo,' said Kyros, who had been listening.

'Ugh!' The two women pulled faces.

Kyros laughed as he leaned over and kissed his wife's hand. 'Do you want to go back soon?'

Their eyes met in a moment of complete understanding. 'Yes, please.'

'Shall we see you tomorrow?' asked Xandros

'Of course,' said Kyros. 'It's our last day and I'm buying you both lunch.'

'Will that be in the little Greek restaurant down by the docks again?' asked Rebecca nervously.

Alice shot her sister-in-law a look of horror. 'Not the one where you both sang?'

'We will see,' said Kyros—with an air of devilment in his eyes as he glanced over at his twin. 'Okay. Let's go, *agape mou.*' He wanted to take his beautiful wife back to their hotel and to make long love to her as the lights of the city went on outside their window. And afterwards they would lie in bed and he would know the true meaning of the word peace.

The two men embraced as they said goodbye— and even this no longer felt bizarre, because Kyros was no longer afraid to show emotion. He had learnt that a man could still be a man—even if he had a heart. And there was one person responsible for the many joys in his life today. His blonde, beautiful Alice.

They stepped outside into the crisp, autumn air. Golden-brown leaves were already beginning to swirl from the trees in Central Park and Kyros caught Alice in his arms and looked down at her, his black eyes glittering.

'Have I told you today how much I love you?'

She pretended to frown. 'Actually, I don't remember.'

He smiled, his mouth tenderly brushing hers. 'Well, then—let me begin. Alice Pavlidis, I love you.'

And Alice smiled back and tucked her gloved hand through his arm as they started to walk across the park together.

0408 Gen Std HB

MILLS & BOON
Pure reading pleasure

MAY 2008 HARDBACK TITLES

ROMANCE

Bought for Revenge, Bedded for Pleasure *Emma Darcy*	978 0 263 20286 1
Forbidden: The Billionaire's Virgin Princess *Lucy Monroe*	978 0 263 20287 8
The Greek Tycoon's Convenient Wife *Sharon Kendrick*	978 0 263 20288 5
The Marciano Love-Child *Melanie Milburne*	978 0 263 20289 2
The Millionaire's Rebellious Mistress *Catherine George*	978 0 263 20290 8
The Mediterranean Billionaire's Blackmail Bargain *Abby Green*	978 0 263 20291 5
Mistress Against Her Will *Lee Wilkinson*	978 0 263 20292 2
Her Ruthless Italian Boss *Christina Hollis*	978 0 263 20293 9
Parents in Training *Barbara McMahon*	978 0 263 20294 6
Newlyweds of Convenience *Jessica Hart*	978 0 263 20295 3
The Desert Prince's Proposal *Nicola Marsh*	978 0 263 20296 0
Adopted: Outback Baby *Barbara Hannay*	978 0 263 20297 7
Winning the Single Mum's Heart *Linda Goodnight*	978 0 263 20298 4
Boardroom Bride and Groom *Shirley Jump*	978 0 263 20299 1
Proposing to the Children's Doctor *Joanna Neil*	978 0 263 20300 4
Emergency: Wife Needed *Emily Forbes*	978 0 263 20301 1

HISTORICAL

The Virtuous Courtesan *Mary Brendan*	978 0 263 20198 7
The Homeless Heiress *Anne Herries*	978 0 263 20199 4
Rebel Lady, Convenient Wife *June Francis*	978 0 263 20200 7

MEDICAL™

Virgin Midwife, Playboy Doctor *Margaret McDonagh*	978 0 263 19894 2
The Rebel Doctor's Bride *Sarah Morgan*	978 0 263 19895 9
The Surgeon's Secret Baby Wish *Laura Iding*	978 0 263 19896 6
Italian Doctor, Full-time Father *Dianne Drake*	978 0 263 19897 3

0408 Gen Std LP

Pure reading pleasure

MAY 2008 LARGE PRINT TITLES

ROMANCE

The Italian Billionaire's Ruthless Revenge *Jacqueline Baird*	978 0 263 20042 3
Accidentally Pregnant, Conveniently Wed *Sharon Kendrick*	978 0 263 20043 0
The Sheikh's Chosen Queen *Jane Porter*	978 0 263 20044 7
The Frenchman's Marriage Demand *Chantelle Shaw*	978 0 263 20045 4
Her Hand in Marriage *Jessica Steele*	978 0 263 20046 1
The Sheikh's Unsuitable Bride *Liz Fielding*	978 0 263 20047 8
The Bridesmaid's Best Man *Barbara Hannay*	978 0 263 20048 5
A Mother in a Million *Melissa James*	978 0 263 20049 2

HISTORICAL

The Vanishing Viscountess *Diane Gaston*	978 0 263 20154 3
A Wicked Liaison *Christine Merrill*	978 0 263 20155 0
Virgin Slave, Barbarian King *Louise Allen*	978 0 263 20156 7

MEDICAL™

The Magic of Christmas *Sarah Morgan*	978 0 263 19950 5
Their Lost-and-Found Family *Marion Lennox*	978 0 263 19951 2
Christmas Bride-To-Be *Alison Roberts*	978 0 263 19952 9
His Christmas Proposal *Lucy Clark*	978 0 263 19953 6
Baby: Found at Christmas *Laura Iding*	978 0 263 19954 3
The Doctor's Pregnancy Bombshell *Janice Lynn*	978 0 263 19955 0

MILLS & BOON®
Pure reading pleasure

JUNE 2008 HARDBACK TITLES

ROMANCE

Hired: The Sheikh's Secretary Mistress *Lucy Monroe*	978 0 263 20302 8
The Billionaire's Blackmailed Bride *Jacqueline Baird*	978 0 263 20303 5
The Sicilian's Innocent Mistress *Carole Mortimer*	978 0 263 20304 2
The Sheikh's Defiant Bride *Sandra Marton*	978 0 263 20305 9
Italian Boss, Ruthless Revenge *Carol Marinelli*	978 0 263 20306 6
The Mediterranean Prince's Captive Virgin *Robyn Donald*	978 0 263 20307 3
Mistress: Hired for the Billionaire's Pleasure *India Grey*	978 0 263 20308 0
The Italian's Unwilling Wife *Kathryn Ross*	978 0 263 20309 7
Wanted: Royal Wife and Mother *Marion Lennox*	978 0 263 20310 3
The Boss's Unconventional Assistant *Jennie Adams*	978 0 263 20311 0
Inherited: Instant Family *Judy Christenberry*	978 0 263 20312 7
The Prince's Secret Bride *Raye Morgan*	978 0 263 20313 4
Milllionaire Dad, Nanny Needed! *Susan Meier*	978 0 263 20314 1
Falling for Mr Dark & Dangerous *Donna Alward*	978 0 263 20315 8
The Spanish Doctor's Love-Child *Kate Hardy*	978 0 263 20316 5
Her Very Special Boss *Anne Fraser*	978 0 263 20317 2

HISTORICAL

Miss Winthorpe's Elopement *Christine Merrill*	978 0 263 20201 4
The Rake's Unconventional Mistress *Juliet Landon*	978 0 263 20202 1
Rags-to-Riches Bride *Mary Nichols*	978 0 263 20203 8

MEDICAL™

Their Miracle Baby *Caroline Anderson*	978 0 263 19898 0
The Children's Doctor and the Single Mum *Lilian Darcy*	978 0 263 19899 7
Pregnant Nurse, New-Found Family *Lynne Marshall*	978 0 263 19900 0
The GP's Marriage Wish *Judy Campbell*	978 0 263 19901 7

0508 Gen Std LP

Pure reading pleasure

JUNE 2008 LARGE PRINT TITLES

ROMANCE

The Greek Tycoon's Defiant Bride *Lynne Graham*	978 0 263 20050 8
The Italian's Rags-to-Riches Wife *Julia James*	978 0 263 20051 5
Taken by Her Greek Boss *Cathy Williams*	978 0 263 20052 2
Bedded for the Italian's Pleasure *Anne Mather*	978 0 263 20053 9
Cattle Rancher, Secret Son *Margaret Way*	978 0 263 20054 6
Rescued by the Sheikh *Barbara McMahon*	978 0 263 20055 3
Her One and Only Valentine *Trish Wylie*	978 0 263 20056 0
English Lord, Ordinary Lady *Fiona Harper*	978 0 263 20057 7

HISTORICAL

A Compromised Lady *Elizabeth Rolls*	978 0 263 20157 4
Runaway Miss *Mary Nichols*	978 0 263 20158 1
My Lady Innocent *Annie Burrows*	978 0 263 20159 8

MEDICAL™

Christmas Eve Baby *Caroline Anderson*	978 0 263 19956 7
Long-Lost Son: Brand New Family *Lilian Darcy*	978 0 263 19957 4
Their Little Christmas Miracle *Jennifer Taylor*	978 0 263 19958 1
Twins for a Christmas Bride *Josie Metcalfe*	978 0 263 19959 8
The Doctor's Very Special Christmas *Kate Hardy*	978 0 263 19960 4
A Pregnant Nurse's Christmas Wish *Meredith Webber*	978 0 263 19961 1